THE MARSHAL'S OWN CASE

THE MARSHAL'S OWN CASE

MAGDALEN NABB

A Marshal Guarnaccia Mystery

CHARLES SCRIBNER'S SONS

New York

Charles Scribner's Sons
Macmillan Publishing Company
866 Third Avenue, New York, NY 10022

Library of Congress Cataloging-in-Publication Data

Nabb, Magdalen, 1947–
The Marshal's own case : a Marshal Guarnaccia
mystery / Magdalen Nabb.
  p. cm.
ISBN 0-684-19201-2
I. Title.
PR6064.A18M35 1990
823'.914—dc20   90-8093   CIP

10 9 8 7 6 5 4 3 2 1

PRINTED IN THE UNITED STATES OF AMERICA

For generous help with the
research for this book I
wish to thank 'Fabiana'
(Gianni Ciardiello).

CHAPTER 1

The week that school opens for the autumn term is as bad as Christmas. That, at least, was Marshal Guarnaccia's opinion. The biggest department store in Florence had, as usual, given over a whole floor to racks of black, white, blue and checked school overalls and all the shelves were stacked with exercise books, pencils, plastic satchels and the like. The place was teeming with harassed parents and demanding children who dodged from stand to stand grabbing for the brightly coloured packages of felt-tipped pens and Mickey Mouse rubbers. Mothers consulted their lists, trying to puzzle out which child needed triple-lined exercise books and which needed double. Fathers put in an occasional protest about the amount of unnecessary money being spent, but without much hope of being listened to. The place was overheated and the noise deafening.

The Marshal had made no protest as yet. He had been plodding around behind his wife and the two boys for an hour and ten minutes exactly. He'd just looked at his watch. At this time of an afternoon he usually dozed over the newspaper, his after-lunch coffee going cold on the little table next to the sitting-room sofa. He'd made no protest about that, either, but now he was beginning to wonder if he'd manage to make it back to the carabinieri station at the Pitti Palace in time to be in his office at five. They'd already stood in a long queue at the cash desk for a good quarter of an hour, only to find that something or other had been forgotten and the three of them were off again, Totò yelling: 'Over here! They're over here!' Teresa kept on telling him to keep his voice down but what the point of that was the Marshal couldn't see, since every other child in the place was shouting. You couldn't hear yourself think, never mind move about in this crowd.

They had disappeared again. He gave up trying to follow them and stood still, his huge, black-uniformed bulk looking like a whale stranded on a swarming beach. A faint 'Oof!' escaped him as he fished for a handkerchief to mop his brow. A running child tripped over his big black shoe and a woman prodded him.

'Are you in this queue or not?'

He dislodged himself from the crowd near the cash desk without answering. There was nowhere he could put himself where he wouldn't be blocking everybody's way. Too bad. As far as he could remember, all he'd ever taken to school was a sheet of lined paper for his weekly composition. Pencils were fished for in the kitchen drawer or borrowed.

'But, Mum! It's miles too long!' A little boy behind the Marshal was protesting as his mother held a black overall against him.

'I'll turn it up. It'll do you next year as well. Will you stand still!'

He noticed that hardly any children bothered with the satin bow at the neck any more. His mother had always made such a thing about getting it just so, tugging at it for what seemed like hours while he struggled to get free and be off down the dusty yellow road in time for a bit of mischief on the way. She used to plaster his springy black hair down with water, too, another thing he'd always hated. And as he shot out of the kitchen door like a wild animal set free, she always followed him to shout in his wake, 'And don't you be playing on the way to school or you'll get dirty! Think on!' He always played on the way and he always got dirty and his mother knew very well that he did but she went on saying it just the same. Now his wife, Teresa, went on saying to Toto, day after day, 'Keep your voice down,' though she knew he was incapable of saying a thing if he could shout it.

'I said no!' A woman's exasperated voice brought him out of his stupor. A little girl beside him was sobbing in front of a stand filled with plastic satchels.

'I can't afford it—we've still to buy all your text-books!'

The mother's voice had no effect on the child, who went on sobbing. She was holding on to the shelf with all her force so that she couldn't be dragged away. A slightly taller girl of perhaps eight or nine stood watching with one of the pink plastic satchels held against her chest. She was a particularly pretty child with very long fair hair and brown eyes. The Marshal was fascinated by the expression on her face which wavered between distress at the other girl's situation and smugness at her own good fortune. The more the smaller child cried, the more she clutched the satchel to herself, her eyes bright.

The Marshal turned away. His own face, with its big and slightly prominent eyes, was always expressionless but, even so, he had caught the fair child's mood. He felt that same tug of distress at the problem all this unnecessary buying must cause for hard-up families, coupled with self-satisfied relief at the thought that he could afford it. At least . . . He fished out his wallet and looked inside, though he had no idea of how much his wife had bought by this time. It was true what that woman had said just now, that there were still text-books to buy. He hoped he wouldn't get dragged along on that expedition. The queue outside the bookshop often stretched the length of the street and even when you got to the front and gave in your list there was another long wait.

Half past four. He was going to be late. He still made no move to find his wife and children. It was easier for them to find him if he just stood where he was. He stood where he was for a further fifteen minutes and then they found him, or rather, Totò did, hurtling at him to shout: 'Mum's right at the front of the queue and she says for goodness' sake come because she's hardly got any money!'

'I'm going to be late,' he said when he'd paid.

'Here, carry this . . . and this. Wait a minute, has she given me the right change . . .?'

'It's quarter to five.'

'No, no, it's right. Don't start grumbling, Salva, we've practically finished.'

'Practically?'

'I just want to stop off on the next floor down. They both need socks. So do you, when I come to think of it. Totò! Will you keep your voice down! We're not buying anything else on this floor and that's final. Hold Giovanni's hand on the stairs and if we get separated go straight to the children's sock counter. Are you listening? Salva, where are you? Salva!'

He plodded down the stairs behind them, his big eyes roving over the heads of the crowd below. He spotted the long fair hair of the pretty little girl who was standing still and patient while something else was bought for her, fussed over by an equally blonde young woman, probably her mother, and a well-dressed older woman who seemed to be directing operations. He remembered the other child who had been so heartbroken because she couldn't have a satchel.

'Don't you think we've bought enough?' he murmured, as they reached the bottom of the stairs, but his wife didn't hear him.

He was late. There was a woman in the waiting-room who half got to her feet when she saw him, but he only nodded to her and went through to his office, knocking on the door of the duty room on the way. With any luck his young brigadier, Lorenzini, would produce a cup of coffee for him. He needed a minute or two to get his breath back. He settled down behind his desk with a sigh, his head still buzzing with the noise of the department store. Lorenzini knocked and put his head round the door.

'Come in, come in.' Then he added: 'How did you guess?'

For Lorenzini had a cup of coffee in his hand.

'I knew you'd all gone shopping and you got back late, so . . . You don't look as though you enjoyed it much.'

'Enjoyed it? Listen . . .'

Lorenzini listened. It was something he was good at. The Marshal sipped the thick, scalding coffee and grumbled.

'And the worst of it is,' he wound up at last, 'that we'll hardly have done spending on this school business before the Christmas decorations will be up and it'll be buy, buy, buy all over again. Yours is only a baby yet, but you'll soon know what I'm talking about.'

He knew he was exaggerating but he couldn't help it. Nor could he tell Lorenzini that what he was really feeling was a bit guilty, and all because of a little girl who couldn't have a satchel and a prettier one who could.

'Most of it's rubbish, anyway. They don't need it all but what one has they all have to have and the shops take advantage. I feel better for that coffee, I must say . . . Who's that woman in the waiting-room?'

'A Signora Fossi.'

'What does she want?'

'To see you. Wouldn't tell me what it was about, just that she wanted your advice.'

'All right. Show her in.'

He stood up as the woman entered the room and offered her a chair. By the time she had taken it and he had gone back behind his desk, he had already decided that it wasn't the usual story of a mother in a panic because she thought her youngster was on drugs. Too old, for one thing. She looked well over sixty. She also looked more determined than distressed. He hoped it wouldn't turn out to be one of those quarrels with neighbours which he hated dealing with. She looked the type for that. She also looked familiar but he couldn't place her.

'Now then, Signora, what can I do for you?'

'I've come about my son.'

'I see. He's in some sort of trouble?' Surely any son of hers must be at least forty.

'You perhaps think it odd,' she said, as if reading his thoughts, 'since my son is over forty—forty-five to be exact —that I should be here rather than my daughter-in-law. Nevertheless . . . We've always been very close, Carlo and I, and I *know* when something's wrong.'

Oh Lord, thought the Marshal, but he only said: 'What exactly do you think is wrong?'

'He's gone.'

'Gone?'

'Missing.'

'I see. Since when?'

'Two weeks ago . . . no, more. It was a Saturday and today's Tuesday. That makes it almost two and a half weeks.'

'You think he's left his wife?'

'I think nothing of the sort, even though . . .'

'Even though what?'

'I was going to say that he had reason . . . but that's nothing to do with it. He wouldn't leave her, not without telling me first.'

The Marshal suppressed a sigh.

'Do you live with your son and daughter-in-law, Signora?'

'Yes and no. We have a small factory. My husband started it and before he died we rebuilt. The house is part of the same complex. It's a large house and I live in a self-contained flat which occupies the whole of the top floor. Carlo lives on the ground floor with his wife and little girl.'

'And he works in the factory?'

'We all do, all three of us. I supervise the whole business since my husband died. My son is in charge of production and my daughter-in-law keeps the accounts and deals with orders. We produce silver giftware.'

'And you say your son's been missing for over two weeks? Surely that must have caused big problems. I don't understand why you waited all this time ... He's not, by any chance, in the habit of disappearing for short periods?'

'I—it has happened.' The woman's face and neck flushed red but her eyes remained steely and determined. The Marshal was glad she wasn't his mother-in-law. The thought prompted him to ask, 'What does your daughter-in-law think? You've talked it over with her, have you?'

'Naturally.'

'So?'

'He's never been gone so long before, never more than three or four days. This time it's different, we're agreed on that, at least.'

'If not on anything else, is that it?'

'I didn't say so.'

'No, no ... I just had the impression that you weren't too happy about your son's marriage—what age was he when he married?'

'Thirty-seven. You're quite mistaken. I not only approved the marriage, I brought it about.'

'Oh.' The Marshal stared at her with bulging, expressionless eyes. 'I didn't think arranged marriages still happened.'

'Of course not. Let's say I did everything possible to encourage my son to marry. My daughter-in-law was already working for us as a designer. I thought she'd make him a good wife.'

'You've changed your mind since?'

She seemed to consider this carefully before answering. 'No,' she said at last, 'she's a hard worker and keeps a good home. Even so, she ought to realize that when a man doesn't marry until his late thirties he's bound to be rather set in his ways ... Besides which, she's from Finland. Their ways are not ours.'

'I take it you're referring to his three-day jaunts,' said the Marshal mildly. 'You can hardly expect her to approve. Where does he go?'

'I've no idea. It's not my place to inquire into his private life.'

'Even though you're so close?'

She tightened her lips and was silent.

'You must have an idea,' he said, 'even if you're not sure. Is there another woman?'

'Certainly not. He's never gone in for that sort of thing.'

'Ah. But he must sleep somewhere when he's away. Does he have a room somewhere, a hideaway?'

'No. I told you my daughter-in-law handles all the accounts. That goes for their private accounts as well as those of the business. He couldn't spend that sort of money without her knowing.'

'Did he take a substantial amount of money when he disappeared?'

'None at all. Except, of course, whatever was in his wallet. And he took no clothes apart from those he was wearing. Surely that in itself is enough to suggest that something's happened to him.'

It wasn't really enough at all. He wouldn't be the first to walk out on his life without a word and never be found again. The world is full of tramps who've done just that. Even so, it would be cruel to say so. Instead, the Marshal asked, 'Have you checked the hospitals?'

'No. I came straight to you.'

'After over two weeks.'

'If there'd been an accident we'd have been informed.'

The Marshal rolled a sheet of lined paper on to his typewriter.

'I need his full name and address and a description. Do you have a photograph of him?'

'Not with me.'

'You'll have to bring me one. Name and address?'

'Fossi, Carlo Emilio, via del Fosso 29, Badia a Settimo, Scandicci.'

'Scandicci?' The Marshal pulled the sheet of paper out

of the typewriter, crumpled it and dropped it in the waste-paper basket. 'Signora, you shouldn't have come here.'

'What do you mean? I've explained—'

'You must go to the carabinieri in Scandicci. I can't deal with this, it's not in my area. Go to your local station with a photograph of your son and they'll publish it along with his description in the research bulletin.'

'And what if my son's left Scandicci? What's the use of its only being published there?'

'No, no, Signora. The carabinieri at Scandicci will send the information to the Questura here in Florence who'll feed it into the data bank and transmit it to the Ministry of the Interior. They publish the bulletin throughout the whole country.'

'If that's the case, then I don't see why you can't do it now that I'm here.'

'I'm sorry, Signora, but I can't do that. I don't understand why you came here at all when there's a carabinieri station not two minutes away from your house.'

'I came here,' she snapped, 'because a friend recommended you.'

'*Recommended* me?' As if he were a restaurant!

'A very particular friend here in Florence. She lives on the via San Leonardo and you settled a dispute over the boundary between her garden and her neighbours'. As I was in town with my granddaughter and my daughter-in-law buying the child's school things, I took the opportunity of staying on and having a cup of tea with her. She suggested I come here. She said you were a sensible man . . .'

She didn't complete the sentence but its implication hung in the air. What's more he'd placed her now. In the department store . . . the blonde mother and child and the organizing grandmother. That little girl wasn't quite so fortunate as he'd imagined!

Two hours later, when the woman was long gone and the Marshal was writing out the daily orders for Wednesday, he was still grumbling to himself. '"A very particular friend"! What a character!'

The fine autumn evening had faded and the lights were on. A wonderful smell of cooking was filtering in from somewhere. He paused in his work to sniff, feeling hungry. Lunch had been a hasty affair because of the shopping expedition. That smell wasn't coming from his quarters or he would have recognized one of his wife's dishes. It must be Bruno cooking for the lads in the kitchen upstairs. They were supposed to take turns with the cooking and shopping as with all their other duties, but Bruno was a good cook and refused to eat the messes that the others served up. The Marshal had given up trying to interfere. The boy would be off his hands before long, once there was a place for him in Officer Training School, and a good thing too. He couldn't cope with Bruno who always left him speechless. Teresa always said, 'That's because he's so intelligent . . .' Another of those unfinished sentences. Well, he'd never claimed to have any brains himself, though he did like to think he was, at least, a sensible man. That awful woman . . .

His reverie was interrupted by a piercing scream from the waiting-room.

'Now what . . .?'

He opened his door. The screams were coming from a small girl of about five who was stamping in fury on a pile of what seemed to be her own clothes, her face swollen and red with the effort. Di Nuccio, one of the two men who must have brought her in in a patrol car, was trying to quieten her. He received a sharp kick on the shin from a tiny but well-aimed shoe.

'Ow!' yelled Di Nuccio.

'She bites as well,' offered the other lad, rubbing his hand and standing well back.

'I don't want you!' screamed the child, 'I want my mum, I don't want you! Go away! Go on, go away!' She aimed another kick but this time Di Nuccio dodged it. Enraged, the child whipped off her shoe and flung it across the room. It hit the Marshal and, for the first time, she noticed him. It might have been his size or, more probably, his huge bulging eyes that were fixed on her, but whatever the reason, she stopped screaming and stood still. Then she marched up to him and clutched his trouser leg.

'Are you his dad?' she demanded, pointing an accusing finger at Di Nuccio.

'We found her trying to cross the road by herself,' Di Nuccio said. 'All we could get out of her was that she'd been left in the Pitti Palace by herself. I suppose her parents lost her in the crowd and are still in there looking for her.'

'I'm telling your dad over you,' yelled the child, wagging a warning finger.

'I told the porter we were bringing her in here, so I suppose somebody will come for her soon. She must have been trying to go home, thinking they'd left her behind, but she doesn't know her address.'

'You go away!'

'We'd better get back out . . .'

'I'm not going with you because you're horrible!'

'The thanks you get,' muttered Di Nuccio as he and his mate went off to resume their patrol.

'I'm staying with you, am't I?' said the little girl smugly, satisfied that she'd won some sort of victory.

'If you put your clothes on, you are.'

She stared up at him, taking the measure of his authority, then went and gathered up the pile of clothing and her shoe. She offered the bundle to him in silence.

'Put them on,' he insisted.

'I can't!' She seemed surprised by his ignorance. 'I've only learnt how to take them off. You have to do it.'

She climbed on to one of the waiting-room armchairs and offered him a foot.

'Hasn't your mother ever told you,' he said, unbuckling

the shoe and letting her wiggle her foot into it, 'that if you pull your shoes off like that without unfastening them you'll spoil them?'

'Yes.' She stood upright on the chair and stretched up her arms ready for the frock. The Marshal's efforts at getting it on were tentative and inexpert but with the help of muffled instructions coming from inside the bodice he managed, at least, not to rip it.

'You've put it on back to front,' observed the child, looking down at herself, 'but it doesn't matter.'

'Bring your coat,' the Marshal said.

'Where are we going?'

She trotted along beside him towards his quarters.

'Teresa can see to your frock.'

'Is Teresa your little girl?'

Teresa was in the kitchen getting supper ready. The boys were sitting at the kitchen table with all their new books and pencils spread out in front of them.

'Clear all that stuff away,' Teresa told them, 'it's nearly ready. Salva, I've put a bit of pasta on for you as well as the meat, seeing that you didn't have much lunch. The boys don't want any but—whoever's this?'

'She got lost,' the Marshal said, 'probably in the picture gallery. Somebody should collect her soon.'

'Well, you are a pretty girl.' Teresa bent to stroke the honey-coloured hair. 'What's your name?'

'Cristina.'

'Well, Cristina, you come and sit here at the table and in a minute I'll give you a nice bit of supper.'

'I'll go and get changed,' the Marshal said.

Subdued by the presence of the boys who were so much bigger and took no notice of her, Cristina sat still and watched their every move as they collected up their belongings. Only when they'd taken the stuff off to their bedrooms did she venture to ask: 'Where will I go to sleep?'

'To sleep? Good gracious,' Teresa said, 'your mum will

come for you before bedtime. But you'll eat some supper, won't you? Now that we're having ours?'

'Are those big boys having some as well?'

'And the big boys as well.'

After a while she frowned and asked, 'Where's he gone?'

'Where's who gone, sweetheart?'

'The man . . .' She clenched her fists anxiously, 'The man who's fat right up to the sky and all black.'

'You funny little thing,' Teresa said, rubbing her head. 'Here, this is his plate right next to yours so he can sit beside you. All right?'

'Yes.'

The child remained silent throughout the meal, keeping an apprehensive eye on the two boys. Only when they'd finished and Teresa offered her a slice of red apple did she say: 'I like staying here. I don't want to go home, only . . . I want my mum! What shall I do?' Then her eyes filled with tears.

The doorbell rang.

'Just in time,' said Teresa, 'I think she's had enough.'

The harassed woman shown in by Lorenzini had two older children in tow. She was as much angry as relieved.

'This one drives me crazy,' she said after thanking them profusely. 'Every time we go anywhere it's the same. One minute she's there and the next minute I look round and she's vanished. The minute she gets fed up she sets off home by herself. I can't take my eyes off her for a second. We searched all the streets near home before thinking of coming back here. Cristina, say thank-you to these nice people for looking after you, then we'll go home and leave them in peace.'

'I haven't eaten my apple,' Cristina said, pulling off the coat her mother had just fastened and climbing back on to her chair.

Half an hour later the Marshal was settled on the sofa in the sitting-room with a small yellow lamp lit and the tele-

vision on. He could hear the boys arguing about something
or other in their room and Teresa moving about, clearing
up the kitchen. As usual, he was staring at the film without
following it properly, though he knew that when Teresa
came in and sat down beside him she would want him to
bring her up to date with the story and be annoyed when
he couldn't. The phone rang and he got up slowly, still
staring at the screen. Teresa was out in the hall before him.
For a moment he remained standing. He heard her tone of
surprise as she answered, but then she said, 'How are you
. . . and the children?' He sat down again, thankful it wasn't
for him.

It was one of those fast-moving American crime films,
dubbed into improbable Italian, and the young policeman
seemed to spend all his time either shouting abuse at his
superiors or in bed with the female suspect. Every so often
it would attract his attention sufficiently for him to emit a
faint grunt of disbelief, then he would lose track again. What
sort of stuff would that be that they were eating out of
cardboard boxes in the car? They seemed to do that in all
these films but they never said what it was. All that steam
coming up in the road was from the underground trains, he
knew that much. One of the boys had told him. Something
they could do with in Florence, that, but he doubted if
it could be done. The minute they started digging the
archæologists would pounce and everything would stop for
years like in the Piazza della Signoria . . . how long had
that been going on? Another dead body. That's four, if not
five. Five . . . Whoever's that chap with the beard? Maybe
the man who was seen coming out of the hotel right at the
start. Teresa was going to want to know . . .

But Teresa was still on the phone, not talking much,
though.

'Mmm. Yes, I . . . no, no, not at all. You did right. Mmm
. . . Mmm . . . I will, don't worry.'

When at last she came and sat down she didn't ask him

anything about the film. She affected to watch it but he could feel her tenseness, and if she didn't even want to know who was who . . .

'What's the matter?'

'Nothing.'

He waited a bit but she still didn't question him about the film so he got up and turned the sound down, then sat down again.

'Well?'

'Nothing, it'll keep until after the film if you're watching it . . .'

'Who was that on the phone?'

'A woman from down home, Maria Luciano.'

'Luciano . . .?' He mentally went through their friends in their home town in Sicily but the name didn't ring a bell.

'Poor woman, she's had so much trouble and with all those children . . .'

'*That* Luciano, that awful family!'

'It's easy to condemn them but with the life she's had—'

'What's the matter, is he inside again?'

'I don't think so, she didn't say. It's her eldest boy she's worried about.'

'I'm not surprised. He was roaming the streets before he was ten, looking for trouble.'

'Even so, he's not all bad. He practically brought up those younger ones.'

'I should think he had to with a mother like that.'

'She had to live. A husband always inside and all those mouths to feed.'

'She wouldn't have had all those mouths to feed if she'd looked for a job instead of getting money the easy way.'

'It's easy enough for us to talk, Salva, but she never had much of a chance. She never even knew her own mother and she was brought up in a home.'

'You seem to know a lot about her.'

Teresa looked faintly embarrassed, the way she always did when she'd been helping somebody on the quiet.

'I used to pass on a few of the boys' clothes to her for the younger ones.'

'Hmph. So what did she want?'

'I told you, she's worried about her eldest, Enrico. It seems he's in Florence. He must be nearly nineteen now. She says he came up here nearly two years ago and got a job in a bar.'

'Well, he probably did right to get out.'

'He'd been sending her money, not regularly but every so often, but she hasn't seen him since last Christmas.'

'And what am I supposed to do about it?'

'I suppose she was thinking you might . . .'

'If she thinks he's inside I can find that out, but if she wants to report him missing she must do it down there.'

'I told her that.'

'You did?'

'The thing is that when he went home last Christmas he was in plaster. It seems he was in a car accident and broke three ribs. Since then she hasn't seen him. He wrote once or twice and sent a bit of money but she was expecting him home for the summer holidays and he didn't turn up. Well, what if he's ill? He might be in need of help.'

'She didn't give him much when he lived at home by all accounts. It's more likely she needs his money and he's stopped sending it.'

'She *is* his mother, Salva.'

'All right, all right. I'll check the prison and the hospitals. But if he's decided he wants nothing more to do with his family, he's over eighteen and there's nothing I can do about it—why hasn't he been called up, anyway?'

'I don't know, but it may well be he was rejected. He was always frail and his chest wasn't too good. You will do what you can?'

'I've said I will.'

'After all, if he works in a bar . . .'

'I can't be going round every bar in Florence.'

'Of course you can't, no. It's just that I can't help thinking . . .'

'Thinking what?'

'If it were one of our boys. Just vanishing like that in another city, how we'd feel . . .'

'All right,' he said more kindly, 'I'll see what I can find out.'

'Perhaps I should have waited until tomorrow to ask you. You've had a long day and one lost child's enough to be going on with. I must say it made me wish we had a little girl—though I should say she was a bit of a handful. Her mother didn't seem to be able to cope with her at all. "Fat right up to the sky"!'

'What?'

'That was how she described you.'

'Hmph.'

'Such pretty hair.'

'She wasn't the first today either. Lost children, I mean. I had a woman in looking for her forty-five-year-old son. Unpleasant sort, too. If her son's anything like her . . . Still . . .' He got up and turned up the sound again, ready for the late news. 'Takes all sorts to make a world . . .'

It was about to be brought home to him just how true that was.

CHAPTER 2

He was standing with his back to a low stone wall gazing down at the scene before him. The grassy slope, littered with illegally dumped rubbish, ended where an olive grove began and, far below that, the jumbled red roofs of the city spread along the Arno valley with the dome and bell-tower

of the cathedral rising in the centre. A blood-red autumn
sunset was reflected in glimpses of the river. Had he taken
his dark glasses off the sky would have appeared pinker and
less ominous, but the Marshal never did take his glasses off
until the sun went down because sunlight made his eyes
water copiously. So he stood there, a large black figure
in a sea of green, watching. He was hungry, but what
Bruno had found he had found just before lunch and
they would be lucky if they discovered the rest of it before
supper.

Bruno himself, unlike the Marshal, was never still for a
moment. He darted from the orange-and-green clad group
of municipal refuse workers to the line of dog-handlers
working their way down the slope, then back again, talking
and gesticulating. Lorenzini, who had been on patrol with
him, had disappeared. Perhaps he was up on the road
behind the wall where the ambulance was waiting and the
Public Prosecutor was talking quietly to the doctor. The
Marshal could hear their voices on the calm evening air. If
any spectators were still hanging around they were as silent
as the Marshal. Once or twice he glanced down at the
contents of two polythene bags lying on a rubber sheet
beside him and then his gaze would drift again to the city
below. He reckoned he must be almost directly behind his
office in the Pitti. A part of the palace was visible through
the trees of the Boboli Gardens. He wondered about Bruno.
You'd have thought a boy of his age—he was only just
nineteen—would have stayed on the sidelines, or even gone
off to hide himself and been sick, but not Bruno. He was
climbing up towards the Marshal now, a little breathless
from his exertions, his eyes bright with excitement.

'They're beginning to think there can't be any more of it
here or else the dogs would have traced it by now.'

'Hmph.'

'You don't agree?'

'Maybe.'

Bruno, too, looked down at the plastic bags but his face registered nothing more than puzzled disappointment.

Lorenzini had called the Marshal at eleven-fifty but he was on the line to Headquarters at Borgo Ognissanti and so he was kept waiting while the Marshal waited in his turn.

'Got anything?'

'Nothing yet.' The man at the other end of the line had fed the name of the missing boy from Syracuse into the computer terminal and was awaiting the response. 'Here it comes . . .' The Marshal could hear the computer spurt out a brief reply and then stop.

'Well?'

'Nothing. No convictions. Anything else I can do for you?'

'No. Thanks, anyway. I'd better check the hospitals but I can do that myself. I've nothing much on this morning.'

But then Lorenzini's call came through.

'I wish I could talk to the doctor,' Bruno said. 'Do you think—'

'No,' the Marshal said, for once not at a loss for a reply to the boy.

'I suppose not.' He was still staring down at the transparent bags. 'I heard what he said, though, to the Prosecutor, about the breasts. It's a very young woman.'

'Yes.'

Bruno crouched down suddenly, peering at the other bag.

'Did you notice? Her nail varnish is freshly done, not cracked or anything. Do you think that's important?'

'I don't know.'

'If only we could find the head. Do you think it was done by a maniac?'

'I don't know.'

'But the doctor said he thought it had probably been done with a saw! It could be a maniac.'

'Yes.'

'What will we do next?'

'Nothing.'

'Nothing?'

'Unless we're asked to do some auxiliary work on the case. It'll be taken over by Headquarters once I've given in my report.'

Bruno looked crestfallen. 'It would be really something, to work on a case like this. Good experience for me. If only I could be the one to find the head.'

And in the event he was. The dogs were moving in a line down the slope and the handlers didn't want Bruno in the way, so he joined the municipal workers who were up on the road on their way to the next blue and white skip. When they started to empty it, he was the one to spot the strands of long dark hair flowing out of a split in a rubbish bag.

The upper part of the trunk, a forearm and hand, now the head. They never found the rest. It was doubtful whether they would have found anything at all if the residents of the houses along the road facing hadn't been complaining for weeks about the illegal dumping of rubbish over that wall. The municipal workers had finally turned up that morning to clear the field and Bruno, who'd been driving the patrol car, insisted on stopping to see what they were doing because their truck was causing an obstruction. A battered suitcase had burst as they threw it in the back along with some mattress springs and a broken chair and Bruno had seen the hand poking out with its red-varnished nails.

It was already dark when they got back. Bruno was still chattering excitedly with no thought in his head of two missed meals. The Marshal's stomach was rumbling, but he switched the light on in his office and telephoned his commanding officer whom he disturbed at supper in his quarters at Borgo Ognissanti across the river.

'Captain . . . Ah, you've heard. Yes, a young woman. No clothing, no identity papers. Can you wait until tomorrow morning for a written report or . . . Thank you, sir. No, nobody missing in my district that I know of.'

And that was that. He went through to his quarters where the boys had already gone to bed. Teresa was in the kitchen, washing up.

'I've saved you some supper as I don't suppose you've had chance to eat anything. Di Nuccio said—'

'I need a shower.'

'Well, there should be plenty of hot water. The boys had theirs before they ate.'

When he came back he was in pyjamas and dressing-gown. Teresa waited a while to see if he intended telling her about what had happened but he sat at the kitchen table forking up risotto in silence.

'It must be a bit spoilt. I wouldn't have made risotto if I'd known you were going to be so late.'

Nothing. Only after a moment did he rouse himself to think of saying, 'It's all right. It's good. Is there another piece of bread?'

She knew better than to force matters. He told her most things sooner or later. In any case, there was something she had to tell him.

'I hope you won't have to be late tomorrow night. There's parents' night at school and it starts at half past six. Do you think you can get away?'

He poured himself half a glass of wine. 'You can go, can't you?'

'Of course, but the thing is, Totò's class teacher telephoned at lunch-time. She specially wants to talk to both of us.'

'What for? Is something wrong?'

'She didn't want to say over the phone, but you know Totò always has more difficulties than Giovanni. In any case, if she went to the trouble to telephone me specially I think we should make the effort. Of course, if you can't get away because you've got something particular on—'

'No, no. I can leave Lorenzini in charge for an hour.'

And she had to be content with that.

Only when they were in bed and she had switched off the lamp did he offer, 'I checked up on the Luciano boy—what's his name . . .'

'Enrico.'

'Hm. He's had no trouble with the police.'

'Well, that's something. I could call his mother tomorrow and tell her.'

'Wait till the evening. I meant to check the hospitals but I haven't had a minute. What was the last address they had for him?'

'I can't remember off hand but it's somewhere in the Santa Croce area. I've written it on the pad by the phone.'

'I might go round there and take a look . . .'

He was still pretty well convinced that the boy had simply had enough of his family, but the day's events had brought it home to him that the nightmarish dreads that assail us all about our children at one time or another sometimes become reality. After all, the three pieces in plastic bags now lying in a refrigerated drawer at the Medico-Legal Institute were once somebody's daughter.

The next day was as beautiful, as calmly sunny, as the last. If it didn't start raining soon there would be a water shortage. It was already being talked about after such a long dry summer. Perfect for the wine-growers who had got in their harvest and were already proclaiming a first-class vintage. The weather would surely break by the end of the month and, in the meantime, the Marshal for one decided to make the most of a fine afternoon and walk over to Santa Croce, the address of the Luciano boy tucked into his top pocket. If he turned out to be still there it would be enough to have a short talk with him, suggest he let his mother know he was alive and well and leave it at that.

Santa Croce wasn't an area he knew particularly well. It

was on the other side of the river and off his beat. His intention was to cross the Ponte Vecchio but as he approached it he saw a gesticulating knot of people blocking the way. It looked as if the 'Wannabuys' were in trouble again. These unfortunates were always in trouble with somebody. They were West Africans who sold their trinkets, belts and bags on the pavements of the city and had been christened 'Wannabuys' by the Florentines because 'wanna buy?' was about the only thing they knew how to say. It wasn't as though they even earned enough to eat, since the vicious organization behind them took most of what they earned. They had trouble enough with the police because they were both illegal immigrants and unlicensed traders, but their worst enemies were the Florentine shopkeepers who saw themselves as the real victims of the situation. This time it was the jewellers whose shops lined the bridge who were complaining. Doing more than complaining, it seemed, as the Marshal drew near. It sounded like one of the jewellers had come out of his shop and assaulted a 'Wannabuy'. The tall white helmets of two municipal policemen were visible in the middle of the violently quarrelling group but they were having no success in dispersing it. An enraged jeweller was shouting: 'If you don't do your job we have to do it for you. Do you know the rates we pay to trade on this bridge? And if I find that shit outside my door again with his junk blocking the way for my customers I'll kick his backside again, do you hear me!' The assaulted 'Wannabuy' was weeping. The others clustered round trying to defend him, their distress more comprehensible than their Italian. The Marshal squeezed past the group and pushed his way through the silently gaping tourists who couldn't understand what was happening but weren't going to miss it anyway.

What sort of unthinkable situation did the 'Wannabuys' escape from in their own country that could induce them to tolerate their life here? Had they left families behind who believed they were making their fortune?

The Marshal crossed the Piazza della Signoria, which was a mass of scaffolding and fenced-in excavations, and made for the church of Santa Croce. There, he had to stop and ask for directions. The street he was looking for turned out to be a very short and narrow one where washing dripped on his head and not a tourist was in sight. Someone was playing the saxophone. There was no Luciano on any of the doorbells but that didn't mean much. He pressed a bell at random at No. 5. The saxophone music stopped and presently a head appeared at a first-floor window.

'What's up?'

'I'm looking for someone.'

'Not me, I hope?'

'Luciano.'

'Not me.' The head vanished and the music resumed.

The Marshal rang again and the head reappeared.

'Now what's up?'

'Come down a minute, will you, or let me in?'

'You'll have to come up. I'm not dressed.'

The Marshal waited and soon the street door clicked open. The narrow staircase was lit by one weak light-bulb and the walls were peeling with damp. The door to the first-floor flat on the left was ajar and the Marshal pushed it open and went in. The small bare room was bursting with music from the rippling saxophone and the face of the young man blowing it looked on the point of bursting too. He ended on a high note with a flourish and grinned. His face was young and round and sunny, his head surrounded by a halo of brown corkscrew curls.

'Have the chair,' he said. There was only one. The Marshal looked around him. Apart from the chair there was a truckle-bed and a small battered table. There were clothes strewn on the floor, a coffee cup and an overflowing ash-tray on the window-sill. The young man wore torn white pyjamas.

'It's not much, and I can't even say it's my own because

I've only got it for a month while the person who lives here is away.'

'The person who lives here isn't a boy called Luciano, by any chance?'

'It's a girl. Why don't you sit down?'

'No, no . . .' He doubted whether the frail wooden chair, pricked with woodworm, would bear his considerable weight. 'I'm trying to trace a boy called Enrico Luciano— he's not in any trouble. His mother hasn't heard from him and just wants to know if he's alive and well. This was the last address she had.'

'Ah, mothers!' He laid the saxophone on the bed as gently as if it had been a child and sat astride the little chair himself. 'I call my mother in Salerno every week, otherwise she'd be up here banging on the door.'

'In that case you know what I mean. Do you know the other tenants in this house?'

'By sight, but apart from me they're all families except for an old pensioner on the top floor. He never goes out because he can't get down the stairs. The woman in the flat next to his does his shopping but I sometimes fetch him a packet of fags when he's run out. He lets a basket down as far as my window and we have a natter. He enjoys the music, says it cheers him up. Nice, that. Some people grumble because I play most of the day.'

'You're a professional musician?'

'You could call it that!' His round smiling face had such a cheerful pink shine on it that it was easy to believe he cheered up the housebound top-floor tenant. 'I play in clubs when I can, and when I can't I go out and play in the streets. Florence is a good outdoor theatre, made for it. I'll stay if I can find somewhere to live . . . Listen, Mirella— that's the real tenant of this flat—has only had it for about six months. She might have got it from this what's-his-name. If you want, I'll ask her when she gets back. It'll be a month, though.'

'You can't get in touch with her before then?'

'Not really. She's a jazz singer—that's how we met—and she's touring round with some group. There's no phone here so she can't ring me. I'm sorry not to be much help.'

'That's all right. I'll leave you to your practising. Just in case she does turn up here's a card with my number—you don't know where she comes from, this Mirella?'

'Sicily, I think.'

'Then you may be right. Luciano's from Syracuse so they might know each other.' The Marshal went to the door. 'Any time you're passing.'

He hadn't closed the door behind him before the music had started up again but when he was going down the stairs it stopped and the young man called after him.

'Hey! you don't happen to know of an empty flat by any chance?'

'No.'

'OK. Just thought I'd ask. You never know!'

And the cheery notes of the saxophone followed the Marshal down the narrow street. Well, he'd done what he could.

Back in his office there was a message from his commanding officer and he was looking at it thoughtfully when Lorenzini knocked and looked in.

'Your wife . . .'

'Salva!' Teresa pushed in, dressed for the street. 'Surely you haven't forgotten? We've to go to the school! We'll look well being late when it's only across the road. Go and get changed, for heaven's sake!'

It was, as Teresa had said, only across the road. The Niccolò Macchiavelli Middle School was housed in one of the palaces facing the Pitti. But when they climbed the broad stone staircase they found long queues outside every classroom and a crowd of parents around a list on the wall telling them where to find the teachers they had to see. It was

Teresa who pushed her way through and copied down the
room numbers on a bit of paper. She seemed to know
all the other parents and had something to say to them all.
The Marshal stood on one leg and then the other and
waited.

'Right,' she said, pushing her way out and consulting her
list, 'the main thing is to see Totò's class teacher. You go
and queue outside Room No. 5 while I try and see some of
the others, but don't go in without me. Giovanni's having
trouble with maths as usual, so I think I should queue there
first . . .'

The Marshal waited outside room No. 5. He recognized
some of his neighbours but only a few of them noticed him
or recognized him without his uniform. After twenty minutes
had gone by and he had edged forward less than a yard, he
began to wish he hadn't put an overcoat on. It was only a
light one but he was too hot, even so, and embarrassed to
take it off. He hardly ever came to the school, and when he
did, the minute he got inside he felt like a pupil again and
started worrying about his own behaviour instead of his
children's. Just the smell of the place was enough to make
him feel eleven years old and teachers half his age could
make him feel inadequate. Maybe people who'd been clever
at school didn't feel like that. The tall woman with glasses
who seemed to be canvassing the parents in all the queues
over some issue or other obviously didn't feel the way he
did.

'If we don't get any satisfaction from the director of the
school I'm prepared to take it further . . .'

It was bad enough facing the teachers, never mind the
director whom the Marshal had never even seen!

'There must be a gymnasium nearer than that. By half
past twelve the children are hungry and a twenty-minute
walk through the crowds in the centre to get to a PE lesson
is ridiculous. It's no wonder some of them are skipping off.
And when you think of all those acres of green right across

from here behind the Pitti Palace and nowhere where the children can so much as play with a ball . . .'

That was true enough. Even so, he wouldn't have the nerve . . . She was probably always top of the class at school. Most of the parents were as meek as himself, he noticed, though they agreed with everything the woman in the glasses had to say. He'd never done more than just scrape through in any subject. Not that he'd suffered much from it, since nobody expected more of him. It was after a parents' night like this—he must have been about nine— that his mother had come home and said, 'They're all sure you could do just a little better if you'd only try and concentrate. You always seem to be in a dream, or else you're thinking about something else.' She hadn't been angry. He knew that she would have liked him to be clever enough to enter a seminary but she never took it out on him when she realized he'd never manage it. She used to say, 'As long as you've got your health . . .' He tried to remember whether he'd deliberately got poor marks because he didn't want to be sent to a seminary but he couldn't recall having any feelings about it one way or another. He edged forward a little as a mother came out of the classroom and another went in. Funny thing, that, about memory. Some things from your childhood, the smell of things, and certain children, stuck in your mind as clear as day but never the reason why you did things. That woman was getting nearer. She was trying to make everybody sign something and he hoped she wouldn't ask him because he wasn't at all clear about what exactly her complaint was—which just went to show that his teachers were right about him! He seemed to be quite near the front of the queue all of a sudden and he hoped Teresa would turn up soon.

'If the parents of all the children concerned sign . . .'

Thank goodness she didn't ask him. She asked the tiny, silent woman standing almost beside him and must have thought he was her husband. He sighed and shifted his weight and wondered where he would be at this minute if his mother had got her way about the seminary. She'd been happy enough when he'd joined up, though, knowing it was a safe, respectable career. He'd never confessed to anybody, not even Teresa, that he really wanted to be an artisan. He was still fascinated by people who had the skill to make beautiful things. He didn't tell because he was conscious of having clumsy hands that were too big and people would only have laughed. He stuffed them in his pockets automatically now as soon as he thought of it.

'Salva! Why ever don't you take your overcoat off, your face is as red as a beetroot.'

Teresa was carrying hers over her arm. He went so far as to unbutton his but that was all.

'How did it go?'

'All right. I managed to see his maths teacher and his class teacher. If we don't get to all the others I don't think it will matter too much. If he can get his maths up to scratch he'll get through. They always say the same about Giovanni, that he's well-behaved and quiet and does his best. It's Totò I'm worried about.'

And so was his teacher when they finally got in there and sat in front of her desk, gazing at her with big worried eyes like two nervous children. She was young and quite friendly, which was a help, but, even so, it seemed that things were going badly for their younger boy.

'It's early in the year, I know, but it's not as though he has such a good record that we can afford to wait and hope he'll settle down later on.'

'He's never been as easy as his brother,' offered Teresa, 'but he's not a bad child, he's just so lively. He can be a bit of a handful.'

'Yes . . .' The young teacher looked doubtful. She hadn't yet made any specific complaint and she seemed reluctant to broach the real problem. 'It's just that—it's not only his work . . .

'How do you mean?' Teresa asked.

'I'm afraid he's got in with a bad crowd. That's why I rang to ask you both to come. I thought perhaps . . .' Her glance moved from Teresa to the silent Marshal whose big hands were placed squarely on his knees. 'There's a small group of boys in the class who are constantly in trouble in one way or another. They're all from fairly rough families and it's only to be expected that they're the way they are. The trouble is that your son's attached himself to them and since he's so obviously not really one of them, he's being led like a sheep and has to go out of his way to prove that he can behave worse than they do. It's the sort of thing that happens fairly often with well-brought-up children who want to be thought one of the lads. But in this case . . . well, they have been known to get in trouble out of school. I just thought it's the sort of thing that could cause you a lot of embarrassment, apart from anything else.' Again, she looked at the Marshal.

'What sort of trouble?' he asked.

'Oh, nothing too serious. There have been one or two complaints from the shops here in the square, for example. They go round them all asking for stickers, you know the sort I mean, the little coloured trademark stickers you see on shop windows and doors. They collect them. As I said, it's nothing serious, but some of the smarter shops don't want children of that sort running in and out. I'm not suggesting you take that in itself too seriously, but I do think we should try and find out why he's taken up with these boys at all. It's not like him and I do feel it's a sign that there's something wrong. I suppose he never brings any of them home?'

'No, never,' Teresa said. 'Giovanni sometimes has a friend in after lunch. They do their homework together, but not Totò.'

'I thought not. They're not the sort he'd want you to see. Does he go out much himself?'

'He does sometimes go out but he always says he's going to Leonardo's house to do homework with him. There seemed no harm in that. He did the same all last year, so I never thought . . .'

'But he doesn't bring Leonardo home with him any more?'

'He doesn't, it's true . . .'

'I thought not. He never bothers with Leonardo any more. I think you should find out where he's really going and perhaps even keep him in—it's a difficult decision to make because setting yourselves against the friends he's chosen can have a negative effect. Nevertheless, the fact that he never brings these boys home or even mentions them to you means that he must be ashamed of his association with them. I don't want to worry you too much but I do think we should find out what's wrong, why he's doing it. It's out of character and I'm afraid he must be very unhappy for some reason. I thought you might have noticed at home . . .'

The two of them sat silent, trying to remember anything different about Totò, but they couldn't. Both their faces were a little red. It wasn't comfortable to be told something about your own child that you were completely unaware of. They felt crushed. And yet, the Marshal thought, why was it that parents were always taken by surprise like this? He'd done any number of things himself that would have horrified his mother if she'd ever found out, but she hadn't. So why was it so impossible to believe that Totò did things they knew nothing about?

'We'd better have a talk to him,' Teresa said, recovering herself first.

'If you don't mind my offering advice,' the young teacher said gently, 'I wouldn't come down too heavily on him. It could make him worse. I don't know whether it wouldn't be better to avoid mentioning those boys at all. You could just keep him in on the grounds that he's behind with his work and needs to study more. That's certainly true. And we should keep in touch. Watch him, and try to find out what's making him unhappy and causing all this.' She glanced at the door where the next parents in the queue were peering in, wondering what was taking so long.

The Marshal stood up. Teresa seemed rooted to the spot, reluctant to leave without having solved anything, without even understanding. Nevertheless, she stirred herself when she saw him standing. They thanked the teacher and left.

They crossed the road and walked up the sloping forecourt towards the Pitti Palace in silence. Only when his wife was unlocking the door of their quarters did the Marshal murmur, 'Should I talk to him?'

'I don't know. It might make it seem too serious. After all . . .'

They went in without her finishing the sentence, she didn't need to. She was always the one to deal with discipline, and her threats of 'if I have to tell your father you'll get a hiding' never came to anything.

'I suppose you're right.'

'We'll have supper first, anyway.'

It wasn't a happy meal. Nobody spoke except to ask for the salt or be offered a second helping. The Marshal ate without knowing what he was eating. You did everything you were supposed to do for your children, worked for them, fed them, clothed them, sent for the doctor when they were ill, and all the time they weren't really just 'the children' they were people, quite separate from yourself. He knew it was ridiculous but he felt as if Totò had given him a kick in the stomach and instead of feeling concerned he felt hurt. It was just as well that Teresa was going to deal with it. Maybe mothers felt things in a different way. That woman, whose name he'd by now forgotten, who came to report her son missing and he was forty-five years old . . . 'We've always been close.' Did it never wear off then, this feeling that your children were just your children and not people? Not even when they grew up?

'Do you want anything else, Salva?'

'No.'

'In that case, I'll clear away.' She gave him a significant look and indicated Giovanni.

The two boys made to go off to their room and he was so slow on the uptake that it was Teresa who had to say, 'Giovanni, stay with your dad a minute, he wants a word with you.'

Totò shot off to the bedroom and Teresa cleared the table and then followed him.

'What is it?' Giovanni asked, puzzled at seeing his father turn on the television and sit down in front of it.

'What?'

'Mum said you wanted to talk to me.'

'Mm.' He got up again and turned the sound down. 'Sit here with me.' After all, Giovanni might know what was wrong, even if they didn't.

'I'm not in trouble at school, am I? The maths teacher said—'

'No, no . . . You're not in trouble . . .' It didn't seem right to talk about Totò behind his back but, after all, Giovanni spent more time with him than anybody else. He might know what was the matter.

'It's Totò we're worried about. His teacher thinks . . . She says he's got in with a bad crowd. Do you know who they are?'

'I know one of them, the one called Innocenti. I don't know his first name. He has a gang.'

'And is Totò in this gang?'

'I don't know . . . maybe.'

'Well, have you seen him with them or not?'

'Sometimes at break. They play cards.'

'Cards? Not for money?'

'A hundred lire or something. I don't know. I don't go near them. Innocenti's dad . . .' Giovanni eyed his father sideways, reluctant to continue.

'What about him?'

'He's in prison. At least, that's what everybody says.'

The Marshal digested this piece of information in silence. He wondered how Teresa was getting on. He couldn't hear a sound from the boys' bedroom.

'Can I go?' Giovanni asked, 'I've not finished my homework.'

'No, wait. Do you think . . . do you think Totò's unhappy?'

'Unhappy? Why should he be? There's nothing wrong with him.'

'No, no . . . it was just something his teacher—no, of course there's nothing wrong with him.' He was well-dressed, well-fed and looked after. What could a teacher who only saw him for a couple of hours a day know about it? He had nothing in the world to complain of. The trouble was that kids never knew when they were well off. When he thought of his own childhood . . . He'd been luckier than most but so many children went without shoes and never got a square meal. He remembered all the money they'd spent at the beginning of term . . . and that little girl crying for a satchel. Perhaps the boys were spoilt and that was the problem. But there was plump, quiet Giovanni beside him, trying now to catch what was being said on the television, and he never got in trouble. He thought he might as well turn the sound up since they were sitting there saying nothing, but then Teresa came back so instead he said, 'Go and finish your homework.'

Teresa took the boy's place on the sofa.

'What did he have to say for himself, then?'

'Nothing much.' Teresa looked unsatisfied. 'I took the teacher's advice and just told him his work was below standard and he'd have to stay in every afternoon and study. I didn't mention the other business. Even so, there was no getting anything out of him. I tried asking if he was unhappy at school, if he felt his teacher didn't like him, if he didn't feel well and so on. He hadn't a word to say—except, as

usual, that we always pick on him and Giovanni's always
the favourite. He was just saying that for the sake of saying
it. I have a feeling that teacher was right. There *is* something
wrong but he's hiding it.'

'Well, there's no point in sitting here all night trying to
guess what it is. I suppose it'll come out sooner or later.'

They watched television for a while, or pretended to. But
the Marshal knew they were both more disturbed than
they wanted to admit. It wasn't long before they gave
up the pretence and went early to bed where they lay side
by side in sleepless silence until Teresa said, 'You're not
worrying about him, are you? It'll be something and
nothing.'

'Of course it will. I wasn't worrying. I was just remembering I've got to go over to Borgo Ognissanti tomorrow first
thing. The Captain wants to see me but in his message it
didn't say why. That's what's worrying me.'

It wasn't, but once he'd produced it as an excuse it began
to.

CHAPTER 3

Captain Maestrangelo was a serious man. The Marshal had
only very rarely seen him smile, and when he did it was
such a fleeting smile and so instantly replaced by utter
solemnity that it was difficult to believe he'd not imagined
it. He wasn't showing any signs of smiling now, but what
exactly he was showing signs of the Marshal couldn't
fathom. So he sat there in silence, his big hands on his knees,
his big eyes watchful but fixed not on the Captain so much
as on a gold-framed oil painting just behind his head.

'I imagine you'll need more men. I can spare you two on
a regular basis—you've nobody off sick?'

'No . . .'

'Then put one of your own lads on the job as well and with my two you should be able to manage. Your brigadier's capable of taking your place when necessary.'

The truth had dawned but the Marshal was having difficulty believing it.

The 'pre-packed' body, as Lorenzini had christened it, had been found on his territory by his men, but a case like that, needing a number of men and a lengthy investigation, would normally be dealt with from here at Headquarters, the Marshal himself giving any local assistance that might be called for. The Captain was within his rights to do what he was doing, but even so . . .

'You want me to lead the investigation?'

'Certainly. You're more than capable of it.'

What the Marshal wanted to ask was 'Why?' but it wasn't his place to ask that sort of question of his commanding officer so he said nothing. Nevertheless, his eyes, bulging rather more than usual, were eloquent with the unspoken question and the Captain avoided them. The answer was not long in presenting itself, anyway.

'I had a call yesterday afternoon from Professor Forli.'

'He's already done an autopsy?'

'Only the first stage. He can't give me anything further on the cause of death yet as he hasn't examined the internal organs. But what he did find out he thought he should communicate right away because it will affect the direction of our—your inquiry. He opened the thorax yesterday and got a surprise. To be more exact, he opened the left breast, then the other to make sure. He says he never would have believed it, he would have excluded the possibility from the size alone. However . . . the breast was a bag of silicone. So, there it is. Not the body of a young woman but of a young man. Obviously, this means the point of departure for your inquiry must be there. The transvestite prostitute contingent in the city is large, but closely knit and virtually closed to outsiders. They all know each other, so at least you'll have no trouble working out which one is missing and getting this . . . creature identified.'

And there it was, the reason. What was veiling the Captain's dark and solemn eyes was distaste. No doubt it was reflected in the Marshal's own face as he began, 'I don't know much about—'

The Captain rose at once and took a small stack of files from a cupboard. He placed these on the desk between them and sat down again. There was nothing else on the broad polished surface of the desk except an unused blotter in a leather case and a heavy glass ashtray, also unused. The Captain was a fastidious man. In the Marshal's private opinion he ought to marry, have children, allow a bit of human disorder into his life, but his face was expressionless as ever as he listened to what he was being told.

'These are the files on all the transvestite murders in the city, or to be more precise, murders committed in and around their world. In some cases the prostitute himself is the victim. Others were probable clients, others again Peeping Toms who may have been seen as a threat by some client who didn't want to risk being discovered because of having a wife and children or a respectable job. A number of them occurred in the Cascine as that's the park where there's most transvestite traffic. As you'll see, all the victims were either battered to death with a handy stone or stabbed with common or garden kitchen knives. There's never been a case like the one you're handling, where the body was cut up and concealed, and before you can find out where the killing took place you'll need to identify the victim so as to know where he operated, whether in the Cascine or at home.'

The Marshal stared at the files one by one. He was dismayed, not by their contents but by their covers, each of which had one word written large in red: Unsolved.

*

The globular white lights along the length of the avenue barely lit the road they were cruising along. They seemed rather to emphasize the blackness beyond it on either side. Every so often a ghostly figure appeared near a tree or a bench, then dissolved into darkness again as they passed by. Some of the figures moved slightly, thrusting themselves into visibility or turning their heads slightly, but the effect was still that of statues placed at intervals. The slow-moving cars which passed in an endless stream, sometimes settling into a queue in front of one of the pale figures, added to the sense of being in some crazy museum without a catalogue and little more than a torch to find your way about.

The Marshal, hunched silently in the civilian car, found it claustrophobic. So much activity taking place with so little light and all of it confusing. Ferrini, the Captain's man, was driving and he, thank God, knew his way about. Even so, it was bizarre and not at all what he had expected. When the Public Prosecutor had directed them to sift through the transsexual population, the Marshal had imagined a road block, lights, uniformed men, anything but this creeping around in civvies at three in the morning, one more kerb-crawling car among the hundreds of others. Where did they all come from? Out of town, a lot of them, to judge by the number plates, but there were plenty of Florentines, too. There must have been more traffic than there ever was in the daytime.

Ferrini slowed and wound down his window. A white figure standing beneath a tree came to life and glided forward. The Marshal caught a glimpse of long pale thighs, white lace barely covering a thrusting pair of breasts. Then a white fur swept down over it all and a face appeared. A man's voice murmured gruffly, 'It's you . . . I didn't recognize you.'

'You weren't meant to,' Ferrini said. 'We don't want to frighten your customers away.'

'What's up, then?'

'Plenty. Listen, is anybody missing off this patch that you know of? That tall one, for instance, the one who's usually over there by the railings?'

'Carla? She's got the 'flu.'

'You're sure?'

'Positive. She's a friend of mine and anyway we ate together this evening. She could hardly eat a thing she had such a temperature.'

'Anybody else?'

'Missing? Not that I know of, but I keep myself to myself so any number of people could be missing for all I know. You get some funny people on this game, I can tell you. I just stick with my own few friends. You know what I mean?'

'Well, take my advice. Stick even closer to your friends than usual. Pair off with somebody. Take precautions, you know how.'

'Has somebody been attacked?'

'Murdered. And nastily. Read the paper. And in the meantime, take precautions. Think on.'

They moved away. The Marshal turned to look out of the back window and saw the white figure staring after them uncertainly.

'You think he'll take your advice?' he asked Ferrini.

'Oh yes, at least for a week or so. They always do. Work in pairs so one can take the number of the car the other gets into, that sort of thing. Soon wears off though, since they know well enough what a risky job they're in. Mind you, a body chopped up like that'll give them something to think about . . . Let's hear what Titi has to say.'

He braked and poked his head out the window.

'Fish not biting tonight, Titi?'

More thighs, this time with black suspenders, and all the Marshal could think of was how cold they must be. For goodness' sake, it was two in the morning and he was in a car with an overcoat and scarf on and the heating turned on full. But each time Ferrini wound the window down he felt the cold. All these people were practically naked!

Titi's head was dark and curly, his lips full and red, a black choker encircled a thick neck.

'After all these years,' he said, wafting heavy perfume in through the car window, 'I knew you'd fall for me in the end.'

'If I ever get the urge,' Ferrini said, 'you'll be first on my list.'

'Don't knock it till you've tried it. I suppose something's up or you wouldn't be here.'

'Where did you get that ring, for a start?' Ferrini asked, glancing at the hand clutching the lowered glass. The hand with its long, varnished nails had three or four rings on it, but one was a very large cluster of what looked like real diamonds.

'Oh God! Not that old story.'

'You tell me. Got a receipt for it?'

'Have I hell got a receipt for it! Do you keep receipts for every piddling thing you buy?'

'I can't afford piddling diamond rings.'

'Change your job, then.'

'Get in.'

'You're kidding!'

'Get in. And think yourself lucky. Worse could happen to you if we leave you here.'

It was as if he'd touched off a fuse. He got into the car all right but spitting with fury. Both the abuse and the perfume hitting them from the back seat were overpowering.

'Shut up, Titi,' Ferrini suggested, 'or you'll be done for abuse to a public official, you know that.'

'I've no right to call a shit a shit, have I, not being a human being like you! Why don't you take a walk up the Via Tornabuoni and stop one of those rich bitches on her way into Gucci's. Ask her for the receipt of all the jewellery she's wearing and see what happens. I work for my money, you know that? *Work!*'

'Shut up, Titi,' repeated Ferrini mildly, 'there's worse things happening in the world. One of your little band's been murdered, chopped up in little pieces all neatly packed in plastic bags. You're safer with us tonight then out working.'

'You're making it up.'

'Not me. You ask the Marshal here.'

Titi didn't, which was just as well. The Marshal, never loquacious, was totally out of his depth and struck dumb.

'So,' Ferrini went on, 'any of your little friends missing?'

'I don't think so . . .' The fury, so suddenly ignited, had evaporated on the instant. He seemed as easily distracted as a fractious baby.

'Anybody at all who's not been around for a day or two, whatever the reason?'

'You expect me to help you? In spite of—'

'That's right. Help yourself more likely, unless you fancy ending up in pieces in a plastic bag yourself. Could have been one of your clients and your turn next. Now, come on, let's hear it.'

Titi gave a little grunt of disgust. When the Marshal turned to look he was gazing out of the window as if thinking of something else but he suddenly leaned forward and tapped Ferrini on the shoulder.

'Gigi's not there, she should be by that bench.'

They drove on slowly and another figure glided forward, sliding a bare leg out from under fur wraps for their inspection.

This time it was Titi who opened his window, calling in a low, drawling voice, 'Hey . . . Mimi, come here a minute . . .'

Mimi, recognizing Ferrini, muttered, 'Oh hell!' and covered the bare leg.

'There's been this dreadful murder,' Titi warned sententiously, 'and Gigi's not at her place.'

'So what? She went to Spain with that bitch Lulu. They were both booked in at the clinic three days ago.'

'Anybody else missing?' put in Ferrini.

'I don't know . . . Paoletta, but she went down to Sicily, her grandmother died.'

'Nobody else?'

Nobody else. They drove on, repeating their question, sometimes forced to queue for ten minutes or a quarter of an hour behind a line of cars while their quarry emerged and retreated, argued, cajoled, and more often than not ended with a shake of the head, sending a car on its way and letting the next one approach. They seemed to turn down nine offers out of ten and only once, after waiting what seemed an age, did a half-naked figure climb into one of the cars to be driven away just as they got near the front of the queue.

'Damn . . .' Ferrini drove on along with the other disappointed clients. 'Well, we'll pick him up tomorrow morning along with anyone else who hasn't shown up tonight. We've got them all listed.'

'That's right! Like we were criminals! Listen, I've never had the slightest brush with the law—'

'Me neither. And what we do's not against the law, is it? Well, is it? Some of my best clients are lawyers—and some of them are cops, too!'

For they now had two passengers filling the small car with two conflicting perfumes and two intermingled streams of abuse. They didn't get back to Borgo Ognissanti too soon for the Marshal. The other two cars on the job had got in before theirs and deposited their haul in one of the larger offices. Ferrini added their two. The noise was deafening. The Marshal hung around near the door feeling useless and deeply embarrassed. It was his habit, when not doing anything in particular, to stand stock still, with his bulging expressionless eyes fixed on some undefined point in the middle distance. It wouldn't do here. No matter where his gaze rested it was bound to be met by some of that bare ambiguous flesh, its femininity so brusquely contradicted

by quarrelsome male voices, one of which suddenly ad-
dressed him.

'Is looking enough or you want to touch?'

'Keep your mouth shut,' warned his nearest neighbour.
'What's the use of getting yourself into trouble for no
reason?'

'I'll say what I feel like! Just because we've been dragged
in here like a bunch of crooks doesn't mean I've no right to
speak. Hey! Ferrini! If a nun gets murdered I suppose you
break into the convent at three in the morning and drag the
other nuns round here for a going-over, right?'

Ferrini looked up from his desk where he was going
through the papers of a huge, silent blond.

'Shut up, or you'll wait till the last if not longer.' He lit
a cigarette and carried on quietly, showing no sign of ill
humour, only rubbing occasionally at his weary eyes.

'Name.'

'Giulietta.'

'Your real name.'

'Fabiano, Giulio.'

'Haven't seen you before. How long have you been in
Florence?'

'Since the summer.'

'Before that?'

'Milan.'

'Address—what the devil's the matter now?'

A quarrel had broken out in one corner of the room and
it was turning into a hair-tearing fight.

'Marshal, do you mind?'

By this time all the others were joining in, shouting at
the tops of their voices. They all seemed to have it in for a
rather undersized creature sporting a pile of upswept chest-
nut curls. As the Marshal stepped forward slowly, mortified
at the thought of having to touch any of them, somebody
snatched at the topknot of curls, which came away leaving
behind a head of straggling black locks. All the others roared

with derisive laughter and the one who had recently made an attack on the Marshal turned on him again now to protest.

'Look at him! A dirty little transvestite! Look at the beard under all that make-up! I refuse to be in the same room as a nasty little pervert like that! Well? Look at him!'

Baffled, the Marshal turned uncertainly to Ferrini who suggested: 'Take him next door, will you, or we'll have no peace.'

The straggly-haired boy was snivelling. The Marshal led him away pursued by hoots of derision.

'You want to lock him up! There ought to be a law against men who go about dressed as women!'

'Trying to pass himself off as one of us!'

'Must be some sort of nut!'

The Marshal shut the door on the racket, relieved to have an excuse to escape. The office next door was dark and empty. He took the boy in there and switched the light on.

'Sit down.'

He sat down himself and regarded the snivelling boy. He was a pathetic sight enough denuded of his curls; his beard was visible as his catty accuser had pointed out. His lips were smudgily painted and mascara was running down his cheeks mixed with tears.

'Bitches,' he said, wiping his nose with the back of his hand.

The Marshal, who had understood nothing of what the quarrel was about, offered him a handkerchief in silence.

'Thanks. I've a right to earn a living same as them, haven't I? Well, haven't I?'

'Do you?'

'Eh?'

'Do you make a living?'

'Enough to manage. I can pay my rent and eat. Nothing to compare with *them*.'

'Hmph.' He didn't understand what the difference was.

He stared at the boy. As far as it was possible to tell, he did have breasts under his cheap short frock but the only difference that was clear to him was that those large doll-like perfumed creatures next door had something theatrically grotesque about them which terrified him, while this kid was only pathetic.

'Couldn't you get some sort of job, an ordinary job?' he asked.

'I did have one but it wasn't enough to live on so I got fed up. What's the difference, as long as I can manage?'

The Marshal gave it up.

'Documents.'

'They're next door on the other chap's desk—you won't make me go back in there?'

'No.' The Marshal had no wish to go back in there himself so there was no danger of that.

'They can get really vicious, some of them.' He had stopped crying and was now rubbing away the mess of lipstick, mascara and tears with the Marshal's handkerchief. When he finished he offered it back.

'No,' the Marshal said hastily, 'keep it.'

'You haven't got a cigarette, have you?'

'I don't smoke.'

'I never carry anything with me except my documents and I keep them inside my clothes. Once I was robbed by a client, do you know that? People say that we're the ones who do that sort of thing and it's true that it happens sometimes, but I've never stolen a penny from anybody. People have no idea what somebody like me has to put up with—once a man tried to strangle me. I got away because we were out in the open, in the park. If we'd been in his car he'd have killed me. I don't like getting in their cars if I can help it, it's dangerous.'

'It's also against the law.'

'Eh?'

'Obscene act in a public place. You should know that.'

The boy shrugged. 'In the park at that time of night? Who's to see? Anyway, it's still a public place whether we're in the car or out of it.'

'You never take them home?'

He shook his head. 'My landlord lives above me. I don't want to lose my flat, and anyway, I share it with two others, so . . .'

'This man who tried to strangle you—when was this?'

'Last summer.'

'You know that somebody's been murdered?'

'No.'

'Why do you think you were brought here?'

He shrugged again. 'How should I know? Listen . . . I don't feel so good . . .'

It was true that his limbs were shaking and he was looking pale and sickly now that his face was cleaner. The Marshal stood up and went round to him, taking a grip on his wrist and looking hard into his eyes. Then his huge hand turned the puny arm gently to expose the needle scars on the inside.

'Let me go.'

The Marshal let him go and sat himself on the corner of the desk. 'Not just rent and food, then. This as well.'

But the boy's attention was drifting as his need increased.

'Will they give it me back? It was only enough for me and I need it . . . You could get me some anyway. There's plenty here, I know that.'

'You do?'

'I know they keep plenty here, to give to informers. I've heard. For God's sake . . . I feel sick!'

To the Marshal's relief Ferrini knocked and came in.

'I'm about finished. Here.' He gave the boy his identity card. 'Hop it.'

The boy stood up but didn't leave. His eyes were fixed on Ferrini, pleading.

'Hop it,' repeated Ferrini, 'before I change my mind and charge you.'

The boy emitted a faintly audible groan and slunk out.
'He'll likely find what he needs before dawn,' observed
Ferrini. 'Shall we go back next door?'

'How much stuff did he have on him?' the Marshal asked
as he switched off the light.

'Too much for it to be his own. Kids like him are often
used as small-time pushers, selling to their clients. But
what's the use? The prison's choc-a-bloc and putting him
inside would only serve to shorten his life. By the look of
him he hasn't got much of a life expectancy as it is—Lord,
what a stink of perfume. I'll open the window.'

They sat down together at the desk and looked at the
results of their night's work: a list of names and addresses,
a packet of heroin and a large diamond ring.

'It was stolen, then?'

'The ring?' Ferrini laughed. 'Yes and no. It's listed as
having been stolen from a very well known Florentine
jeweller. On the other hand, the very well known Florentine
jeweller is a regular customer of Titi's—I've seen them
together in his Mercedes many a time. No doubt he thought
he could be clever enough to make Titi a fancy present and
claim it on his insurance.'

'What will you do?'

'Give it back to him and leave the rest to Titi, who was
none too pleased, I can tell you. He'll get it in the neck next
time they get together.' Again he laughed. 'It's a rum world!'

He fished in his pocket and pulled out a rather squashed
packet of cigarettes. The Marshal watched him light up. He
liked this man, so very different from himself. A relaxed,
comfortable, grey-haired man who laughed so easily and
could chatter away to anybody, even to those . . .

'Is something wrong?'

'No, no . . .' The Marshal pulled himself together. 'I'm
dropping with sleep, to tell you the truth.'

'Not used to these long nights, eh?'

'No, not at all. I was thinking . . . well, it's a good job

you are used to . . . I don't know much about this sort of thing, I don't mind telling you, and as for running this case . . .'

'Oh, you'll soon get into it.'

The Marshal wasn't at all sure that he wanted to 'get into it' but he didn't say so. He only said, 'That quarrel that broke out, for instance, about the boy—'

'Ah yes. Thanks for getting him out of the way or all hell would have broken loose!'

'But why?' the Marshal insisted.

'Why? Because he was a transvestite. They don't think much of transvestites, our friends.'

'I see.' It was clear from the Marshal's large, puzzled eyes that he didn't see at all. 'It's just that, to be honest, I thought they were all transvestites.'

'Transsexuals. Half-way house, as it were. You get some transvestites with these silicone breasts like that kid but they're not on any hormone treatment, still got normal male hormones, body hair and so on and certainly still think of themselves as men. Your transsexual, like our Titi, is a female or reckons to be—only one detail that's anomalous. A lot of them reckon that once they've made enough money they'll have the final operation and retire from business to be fully-fledged females.'

'But . . . some of them seem to have plenty of money now . . .'

'Oh, they have that, plenty. But they can't have their source of income cut off, can they? Their customers wouldn't want them any more.'

'It beats me what they do want . . .' The Marshal's face was red.

'*De gustibus non disputandum.*'

'No, no . . .'

'Right. Well we have a list here of who's missing from the scene. Nobody, at first sight, who seems to be our victim as they've all got a reason for their absence, but we must check all those reasons out. I'll start first thing tomorrow morning with Gigi and Lulu who should be in the clinic in Spain, make sure they're there. Sorry—you should be deciding, but I thought as I know the surgeon . . .'

'Whatever you think . . . What surgeon?'

'The one who does their breasts. They all go to the same clinic in Spain. I've talked to this chap before when I was working on the last two cases, so he knows who I am.'

'Then you do it, yes. How many of these cases have you worked on?'

'Three altogether. Unsolved like this one will be, I suppose, but we have to go through the motions. I'll call the clinic tomorrow. They have to go back there, you see, every so often. It's not a one-off job like their faces. You noticed their faces?'

'No . . .' The Marshal had barely noticed anything, he'd been so embarrassed.

'Noses and cheekbones have to be fined down. That they get done here in Florence; there's a very good plastic surgeon they almost all patronize. Now, there's Paoletta whose real name is Paolo Del Bianco, supposed to have gone home to Sicily for granny's funeral, and this other one . . . where is it . . . Giorgio Pino—another Gigi who, they say, has transferred his operations to Milan. Our chaps up there will know. That leaves Carla. I know Carla, she's all right. Carlo Federico, said to have the 'flu. Only two minutes away from you if you want to go and have a word.'

The Marshal didn't want, but he had to be seen to be doing something. He couldn't leave everything to Ferrini, much as he would have liked to. So he said, 'All right' and was relieved that soon after that Ferrini seemed to think they'd had enough for one night.

He knew, when he got home at half past five in the morning, that Teresa was only pretending to be asleep. But if she noticed that he spent an inordinate amount of time under the shower, scrubbing away at himself as if he'd fallen into a midden, she made no comment. He slept peacefully enough until his usual time of waking, then passed a few uncomfortable hours trying to sleep through the noises of morning, achieving only troubled dreams and a sweaty, aching back. He had another shower.

At four that afternoon, when he presented himself at the appropriate number in Via de' Serragli and rang the bell marked Federico, he was strapped and buttoned tightly into his uniform as if it might protect him from what he had to face. When the door clicked open he went in holding his breath.

'First floor,' directed a man's voice, thick with sleep.

CHAPTER 4

Whatever he had been bracing himself against, it wasn't the pale shiny face, devoid of make-up and a little red about the nose, which peered at him round the door upstairs.

'Federico?'

'That's right. Come in.'

He took his hat off. 'Marshal Guarnaccia.'

'I was expecting you. A friend of mine telephoned me. Sit down, will you? I have to make myself a cup of coffee, I've only just woken up and I feel wretched. Chinese 'flu. Have you had it?'

'Not yet.'

'It's lousy. I won't be a minute.'

The Marshal sat himself down on the edge of an armchair. The sitting-room was small but nicely furnished and very clean and tidy. Two canaries were singing in a cage near the open door to the kitchen where he could see Carla moving about, getting the coffee on. The room was filled with pale November sunlight.

'Do you want a cup?'

'No . . . no, thanks.'

Carla came back, stirring a glass of colourless liquid. 'You'll have to excuse the dressing-gown and slippers. I've been so ill I haven't got dressed for three days and I can't face washing my hair because I've still got a bit of fever.' It was tied back loosely with a scrap of ribbon and some of the dark brown locks had escaped to fall on the pale smooth cheeks.

'Sugar and water,' Carla said, indicating the glass and then draining it. 'My blood pressure's so low . . . the doctor says it's the hormones. Last time it got so low he gave me injections for it but I hate injections, don't you?'

'They're not pleasant,' the Marshal agreed.

'That's the coffee coming up. I'll be right back.'

The Marshal was baffled. He couldn't connect Carla with the wild, theatrical band of last night, and what was more, if it hadn't been for the voice he wouldn't even have been able to tell . . . He felt disorientated.

Carla reappeared with a tiny cup and the aroma of the freshly made coffee filled the sunny little room.

'You're sure . . .?'

'No, no . . . I had mine before I came out.'

'I thought it might be Ferrini who'd be coming. He's all right, is Ferrini, even if he is a carabiniere—no offence meant, only we don't get treated as human beings by cops as a rule, or by anybody else, either, if it comes to that—Mishi! Mishi, come to me!' A glossy little black cat with very bright eyes had crept silently into the room.

'She was fast asleep on my bed,' Carla said. 'She never budges from my side if I'm ill or depressed. Up you come!'

The little cat jumped and settled down with a yawn in the lap of the flowered silk dressing-gown, looking brightly across at the Marshal. It seemed to have a perfectly round head as though it had no ears. Carla held the glossy head gently in large, slender hands.

'He's never seen a cat like you before, has he, Mishi?

Look.' Carla lifted up the black ears with careful fingers. 'She belongs to a special breed. Her ears are folded over so you can't see them. She cost me a fortune and she keeps me on the hop. She'd like to go out, poor thing, but this road's too dangerous. I have to shut her in my bedroom before I open the front door or she'd be out like a shot and it would only need somebody to be going in or out of the street door and she'd be under a car in no time. She once made it as far as the bottom of the stairs and I just got down and caught her in time. Nearly broke my neck doing it, too, didn't I, Mishi? You have to stay at home where it's safe. Poor little prisoner. See how she's staring at you? She's jealous. Sometimes when I bring a client home she makes such a scene scratching at the bedroom door!'

'You bring all your clients home?'

'Always. You won't catch me getting in anybody else's car. You get some real nut-cases at times, you know, on this job.'

'No trouble with your landlord?'

'I don't have a landlord. This house is mine. I have one neighbour who's a constant pain in the neck—she even came here complaining one day that Mishi made too much noise! Can you imagine? A tiny creature like this, you can barely hear her when you're in the room with her! I could understand it if I went in and out at night slamming the door, but Mishi, I ask you! But that's the way people are with us. I'm lucky that it's only that one old bag. The others are all right. What harm am I doing to anybody, when it comes down to it?'

'Perhaps,' the Marshal suggested, 'it's your clients they're afraid of underneath. You say you get some nut-cases . . . You've heard about the murder?'

'My friend told me on the phone. Is it true the body was chopped up?'

'Yes.'

'Christ! It sends shivers down your spine. And you don't
know who she is, the victim?'

The Marshal was about to say it was a he but thought
better of it. 'No, we don't know. That's why I'm here. Is
there anybody missing from the scene, that you know of?'

'No. But then, I haven't been out for a few days. I've seen
all my own friends because they've been round in the
afternoons to see how I am and pick up my medicine for
me, but that's not much to go by.'

'No . . . With a group of over two hundred . . .'

'It's more complicated than that. They're not a group,
do you understand? There are a lot of little groups and they
don't mix, they hate each other. I've been in this game ten
years or more and I can tell you it's complicated. Look, I'm
the way I am and always have been, do you understand? I
don't even need the hormones I occasionally take. It's just
a sort of beauty treatment when I want an extra bit of
plumpness. But there are people who get this way on purpose, just for the money that's in it, if you follow me. Well,
I for one don't have anything to do with people like that—
and then there are the transvestites, people who live as men
during the day and dress up at night like women. Well, I
know what I am but I don't know what they're supposed
to be, do you?'

'No . . . I . . . No.'

Carla tapped her temple. 'Those people have sexual
problems, that's the way I see it.'

'Ah . . .'

'Like a lot of the clients we get—oh, not all of them. I
have some very good regular clients, what I call mature
people, do you understand? They want a transsexual for
fun, for a change, out of curiosity, whatever you like, but
they want a transsexual and say so. You can have a real
relationship with somebody like that. Friendship, a bit of
affection even, but the others—you can't imagine!'

'No.'

'Pick you up pretending to think you're a woman for a start—as if there were any young women on the streets in Florence. Then they act all surprised—but they don't go away, do you understand? They don't go away, they just carry on, still pretending you're a woman. And then—listen to this! Florence is a small place, you know, so then maybe after a day or two you happen to pass each other in the street and he's with his nice little bourgeoise fiancée. Well, a client's a client—he's paid for what he's had and I don't expect more. I don't even look at him in the street, right? But what does he do? He nudges his girlfriend and sniggers and says, "Look at that! It's one of *them!*" They're sick, people like that, sick! And of course there are all the hundreds of homosexuals who can't admit it even to themselves. Wives and kiddies at home and all the rest. But fancy not being able to admit it even to yourself! That's awful, I think, pitiful. So they need somebody like me. There are a lot of people who need somebody like me, Marshal, but only the mature ones admit it. An all-purpose toy is what most of them want, that satisfies their weirdest dreams and doesn't have to be acknowledged as a human being when they wake up. Do you understand?'

'Perhaps . . .' More, at any rate, than he'd understood the night before. 'You've thought a lot about it . . .'

'What else have I got to think about, given the life I have? Or are you surprised I can think at all?'

'No, no . . . I didn't mean—'

'I'll tell you something else. I studied philosophy at university. I graduated, too. But I couldn't go on pretending. I'm made the way I am. It's not very nice to be obliged to dress up as a man when you feel like a woman. I couldn't take it any more so I decided to accept the way I am, only nobody else will accept me. I wanted to be a teacher, do you understand? Do you think anybody will give me a job in this country?'

'I suppose not.'

'You suppose right. And yet they need me and those like me, enough to keep over two hundred of us in luxury in one small city. In luxury, but without any human rights. So I go out of here every night dressed up for the show and I survive—until some lunatic chops me up. That's not my real life. My real life is here, by myself—or with my little Mishi, and my books and records. It's peaceful here. That's what I like.'

It was peaceful. The canaries singing and chattering, the sunlight slanting in through the muslin-curtained window, the little black cat purring. It was a long way from last night's nightmare scene in the park, from the severed limbs on a rubbish dump. But for Carla the nightmare became reality, night after night until, as he said . . .

'Do you know of any client going the rounds who might be really dangerous?'

'Not specially—only you want to watch out for the ones who insist on dressing up as women themselves when they're with us. For me they're the worst sort.'

'Dress up . . .?' This was really one twist too many.

'Wait, I'll show you. Mishi, get down a minute.' Carla rummaged in a drawer of the sideboard and came back with a photograph. 'See that? That's me.' He would never have guessed it and said so.

'It's no wonder. I look a sight now because I'm ill. But mostly it's because I'm dressed up like that. We have to, I told you. It's a show. Anyway, it's that chap in the middle I'm showing you. That's Nanny.'

Nanny was very evidently a man and a robust one who could have done with a shave. Nevertheless he was wearing a woman's evening gown and his lips were inexpertly painted.

'That's an old frock of mine he's wearing. The one I'm wearing I've still got. It's a beauty—cost me over three million. He used to be an occasional client of mine until Lulu got her nails into him. That's her in the middle.'

'But surely, that . . .' He couldn't believe it wasn't a

woman, or rather a girl, since Lulu looked very young. He was posing provocatively in a long sequinned gown open to the waist, turning slightly away from the camera, breasts thrust out, long dark hair falling back over the shoulders, directing straight at the viewer a voluptuous, dazzling smile.

'Not bad, eh? Oh, she's a beauty, all right, is Lulu, but a real bitch, I can tell you. If she ever gets the chop it'll be from one of her own kind. Nobody can stand her except her clients who'll pay anything to have her, though she gives them a hard time, too. Nanny's a fool for running after her. He must have been drunk that night, too, to let himself be photographed like that. Just look at his eyes. He's well away.'

They were certainly bleary but that could just as easily be the effect of the flashlight.

'Well,' the Marshal said, giving back the photograph, 'I don't think it's Lulu who got it this time by all accounts, since they all seem to think Lulu's gone to Spain.'

'Very likely. I wouldn't know. I keep my distance from her.'

'But you were together in the photo.'

'That was a big party—in any case, it was Nanny who insisted. It must be nearly two years ago now. It may even have been that night that he started with her—is that the doorbell? It is. Will you keep hold of Mishi? Otherwise I'll have to shut her in the bedroom.'

The Marshal took the little cat on his lap. It made no objection but sat still, purring gently and watching Carla's every move.

'It's only my shopping. I'm not fit to go out.'

A fat grocer's boy came in with a box of food and placed it on the table.

'How much?'

'Thirty-five.'

Carla was fishing in a brown leather purse. 'Did you put me a carton of cigarettes in?'

'It's there in the corner.'

'Thirty-five. Thanks, Franco.'

'Be seeing you.'

''Bye.' Carla opened the red and white carton. 'I've not smoked for three days. Probably shouldn't now, but still . . .'

'I may as well leave you,' the Marshal said, standing up, still with the shiny little cat between his big hands. 'I really only came to make sure you were alive and well.'

Shaken by a fit of coughing, Carla stubbed out the just lit cigarette. 'That tastes foul. I'm not better yet. Give Mishi to me if you're going. I think I'll go back to bed.'

'It might be just as well,' the Marshal said. 'And if you can afford it you might do well to stay at home a bit longer, until we get our hands on this murderer.'

'Are you kidding? Listen, if I can be of any help, don't hesitate to call me. A lot of the people in this game are out of their minds and would tell you anything, but as for catching whoever did the job . . . It'll be like all the others, once the novelty's worn off things'll go back to normal and it'll all be forgotten. No offence, do you understand?'

What could he say, after seeing all those files marked 'Unsolved'?

'You look like you don't know much about this sort of thing, if you don't mind me saying so. If one of us gets bumped off how much do you think anybody cares? Bit of a thrill reading about a chopped-up body in the papers and we'll probably have more trouble than usual with you people and that's about all it'll amount to. No offence meant, but that's the way things go. Anyway, I've told you, I don't mind a chat any time as long as it's in the afternoon. I sleep in the mornings when I'm working.'

'Thanks.'

'I'll put the light on for you. These stairs are a bit dark.'

He felt he ought to shake hands. It had been a very helpful conversation for him, after all. But his hand lagged behind his feelings and Carla, seeing his hesitation almost before he was aware of it himself, withdrew quickly to save him embarrassment, saying goodbye and shutting the door.

He felt ashamed.

' "One: Time of death approximately three days previously.

Two: Cause of death first of multiple fractures of the cranium, see photographs attached.

Further to the examination of the body *in situ* an autopsy carried out by the undersigned Prof. Forli, Ernesto established as follows:

a) The blows to the head were effected with a smooth wooden object and the first of the seven blows was fatal.

b) The victim offered no resistance to the attack (see (e)).

c) Livor mortis discernible on the lower back and under the forearm indicates that the body lay whole and supine for 10 to 12 hours after death occurred (see (d)).

d) The limbs and head were severed by mechanical means—probably an electrically powered saw—more than 12 hours after death occurred.

e) The contents of the stomach indicate the consumption of a heavy meal immediately before death and the administration of a sleeping draught mixed with red wine.

The above information and the lack of any traces of blood on the site where the body was recovered indicate that the attack took place in another locality and that the body remained there, intact, for at least 12 hours.

General note: The subject, a male, age approximately 20 years, was severely anæmic, a condition attendant on the constant administration of female hormones. As noted in a preliminary report the victim had been given artificial breasts of silicone. As regards the identification of the subject, it should be noted that these weighed 11½ ozs. and that the normal maximum weight would be approximately 8 ozs.

No clothing was recovered for examination but the disposition of the marks of livor mortis indicates that the victim was dressed when the attack took place and remained so until the time when the limbs were severed."'

The Marshal paused in his reading and looked at Ferrini who was examining one of the photographs. 'Shall I read his summary?'

'I don't think you need to. It seems clear enough. Nice meal with a sleeping pill in the wine. A blow on the head once he'd passed out—and then the long wait—why the long wait? An electric saw . . . My God . . .'

'Perhaps he didn't have one,' suggested the Marshal.

'You could be right. I mean, if all this happened at night there are no all-night ironmongers like there are all-night chemists.'

'No. I'd better switch the light on.' They were closeted in the Marshal's office on the afternoon following his visit to Carla. At half past five it was already going dark. The photographs, suddenly illuminated, were sharp and detailed but hardly shocking. It was too difficult to connect them with anything human. Except for the head, of which only a part had been eaten away. It was the head that Ferrini was staring at.

'So it's Lulu,' he said. 'It seemed likely enough yesterday when the Spanish doctor said he hadn't turned up for the appointment, but those eleven and a half ounces tell the story. Eleven and a half ounces, for Christ's sake! He mentioned that on the phone. It's unheard of—and apparently they were giving some trouble which was why he was going back to the clinic. Do you reckon that's sufficient for an official identification?'

'It's a bit unusual. The Public Prosecutor's the one to decide. I suppose I'd better inform him . . .' He didn't know which distressed him most, having to deal with the transsexuals or having to deal with the Public Prosecutor whose attitude from the start had been pretty much the same as the Captain's and who'd even gone so far as to say, 'If people like that kill each other off they're doing society a favour.' He'd said it to the Marshal, of course, not to the newspapers. The last two days' papers were on the Marshal's desk. No pictures of the remains had been released but there was one that showed them, covered by a sheet, on the rubbish-strewn hillside with what seemed to be the Marshal's own feet just visible at the top corner. And in the distance, Bruno. There was no keeping Bruno out of this. He hadn't enough men to pick and choose. At least there was Ferrini, but he couldn't push the Prosecutor off on him.

'Mind if I light up?'

'No, no . . .'

'Are you going to ring him now? Or do you want to wait till we're quite sure?'

'I am quite sure,' the Marshal said, 'I've seen a photo of Lulu alive.'

'You have? How come?'

'Yesterday, at Carla's house.'

'Ah, Carla. Carla's all right. Intelligent. Brutalized by so many years on the game but intelligent underneath.'

'Yes. What Professor Forli said about anæmia . . .'

'They're probably all anæmic. Pale as corpses they are, under all the paint.'

'These hormones they take . . . it seems they lower the blood pressure, too.'

'I wouldn't know, though like as not they're what makes them so unbalanced and hypersensitive. They go up in smoke at the slightest provocation—well, you saw that for yourself.'

'Yes.'

'But Carla's one of the more reliable ones. Maybe you

could get her to identify this head. Not a pleasant sight, mind you.'

'No. I'll ask her for that photo, anyway. The trouble is, there's one of Lulu's clients in it.'

'Cut it. Know who he is?'

'They call him Nanny. Apparently he has a wife and family so he wouldn't have told them his real name.'

'You never know. He won't fancy giving evidence, though, none of Lulu's clients will. It's a non-starter even if he's still in circulation.'

'He is, I think. A regular client.'

'Well, one thing's certain, whoever bumped Lulu off was a client or a friend, not a random maniac. They ate together.'

'From Carla's account Lulu wasn't the sort to have friends. "If she gets the chop it'll be from one of her own kind."'

'Carla said that?'

'Yes.'

'Well, let's hope he's right. We won't have far to look, in that case. Shall we make a move?'

Luigi Esposito, otherwise known as Lulu, lived, or used to live, in the Santa Croce area which the Marshal had visited only a few days before. But the flat they walked into now was a far cry from the bare and squalid bedsitter where the cheery saxophonist was camping. It was quite large and very luxurious. Ferrini gave an appreciative whistle as they opened the sitting-room door.

'Made a good living, our Lulu. I wouldn't mind a stereo like that myself.'

They wandered from room to room without touching anything, waiting for the technicians to turn up. The Marshal automatically went first to the kitchen where the remains of a meal were congealed on dirty plates on a round white table in the middle of the room. If it was *the* meal there was nothing special to indicate it, no overturned chair, no stain of blood. The wine bottle was empty and two glasses still had dregs in them. He would have liked to look in the fridge but it was safer to wait for the experts.

'Marshal? Where are you?'

'In the kitchen.'

'Come and look in here.'

He joined Ferrini in the bedroom. The double bed was unmade, but if the room was in disorder it was the disorder of opulence rather than squalor. The crumpled sheets were silk and the open wardrobe was crammed with obviously expensive clothes, including one compartment bulging with furs. Ferrini sat on the bed and bounced.

'Perfect! And a coloured telly laid on. Videos, too—and I wouldn't be surprised . . .' He jumped up and crouched before the glass shelves next to the television; 'Porn. And very special porn.' He slid a cassette from the collection using his handkerchief and slotted it into the machine. 'There's a shop in the centre rents this stuff out . . . Lord, look at that. Prefer the straight stuff, myself . . .' He sat down on the edge of the bed again and lit a cigarette. 'What language do you reckon that is? German or Swedish?'

'I don't know.' The Marshal turned away from the lurid, slow-moving image and went to look in the bathroom. There was no disorder here. The floor was white marble, the walls white-tiled. There could be no doubt that every surface was spotlessly clean. In the Marshal's humble opinion it was a good deal too clean. It didn't fit in with the kitchen and the bedroom. There should have been more stuff about, more signs of life.

'They're long enough coming,' came Ferrini's voice from the bedroom. 'Christ! Just look at this!'

But the Marshal didn't move. He stayed where he was, staring at the empty bathroom until the doorbell rang and Ferrini went to let the technicians in. Even then he kept himself apart, wandering around the rooms and doing his best to keep his considerable bulk out of the way of electric cables, open boxes of equipment and crouching figures. Nobody bothered to turn off the television in the bedroom and, every now and then, one of the men would pause in his work and park himself in front of it, sniggering or exclaiming. Once they'd finished fingerprinting the bedroom he and Ferrini started going through the drawers and cupboards. It was Ferrini who found a handbag on the floor near the bed.

'Identity card, that's good . . . Hm. Still resident in Naples where he was born, according to this . . . Airline ticket for Spain, even better. Gives us the date of the murder, wouldn't you say? I reckon he must have died that day or the night before, since the others thought he'd gone.'

'Probably. What's that? A receipt from a bank?'

'Looks like it . . . yes. Receipt for payment of traveller's cheques . . . intending to spend a fair bit of money. I suppose that clinic costs but it looks like he was going to make a bit of a spree of it as well . . .'

'Where are they? Are they in there?'

'Wait . . . I can't find them but there's so much stuff in here, junk and make-up—shall I tip the lot out?'

'Yes.'

Ferrini overturned the snakeskin bag and showered the contents on to the crumpled silk sheet. 'I don't know,' he smirked. 'The things men stuff in their handbags!'

'Marshal?' One of the technicians came into the bedroom dragging a suitcase. 'This might interest you.'

The suitcase, when they opened it, was neatly packed with women's clothing, most of it new or nearly so.

'All ready for off,' the technician commented as the Marshal sifted through the clothes, 'but what's interesting is that it was hidden!'

'Hidden where?'

'Pushed behind the sideboard in the sitting-room. Not the usual place to park a suitcase when you're ready to leave.'

'People have their funny ways . . .' said the Marshal doubtfully.

'Funny's right. The sideboard had been moved out to make room for it. It stands on the edge of that Persian rug and there's another set of depressions on the rug from where it normally stands. Didn't want somebody to know he was leaving, do you think?'

'I don't know.' The Marshal went in there and looked at the depressions on the rug but they didn't hold his attention long. Within a moment he was at the door of the bathroom, watching. A young man was taking minute scrapings from between the wall tiles. The Marshal stared for a long time, his big eyes expressionless. Then he sniffed. The bedroom smelled strongly of perfume but the bathroom had a different smell.

'Bleach,' he said at last.

'That's right,' agreed the young man cheerily. 'Spotless. I'm going through the motions but I can tell you I don't expect to find much. No signs of death in this room.'

'No signs of life,' the Marshal said, unconsciously correcting him. Really he was talking to himself and when the young man paused in his scraping and gave him an odd look he turned away, embarrassed, murmuring as if in explanation of his queer remark, 'There are no towels . . .'

Everyone was so occupied, so sure of what they were doing. Everyone except himself. The technicians knew their job and it was pointless to interfere with them. Ferrini knew his job, too. He was busy writing a list of the contents of Lulu's handbag, dropping the things back inside it as he wrote, a Cellophane bag ready to package the whole thing for removal.

'No traveller's cheques,' he said without looking up.

On the TV screen a huge red mouth opened and zoomed slowly forward.

'I'm going upstairs,' the Marshal said. 'Have a word with

the landlady and tell her we'll have to keep the keys and seal the place up.'

The landlady lived on the top floor. He could have taken the lift but he started up the stairs without thinking, so anxious was he to get away from the flat and that wretched television. He arrived on the landing out of breath.

'Oh, it's you again,' the woman said, peering round her door without enthusiasm. 'What is it now?'

Her grey hair was newly waved. She looked sixtyish and aggressively respectable.

'I'd better come in,' the Marshal said. He saw that she was none too pleased but the door opened sufficiently to admit him. He got no further than the highly polished entrance hall but he made no protest about it, standing there hat in hand.

'What exactly is going on?' She was already on the defensive.

'Your first-floor tenant has been murdered.'

She didn't repeat the word questioningly as anyone else might have done, only stared at him as though waiting for some more impressive communication. He was forced to go on without any help from her.

'How long has he lived here?'

'What do you mean?'

'Exactly what I say. How long has he been your tenant?'

'What do you mean "he"? You took the keys of the first floor left. The tenant is a woman.'

'The tenant was Luigi Esposito, a transsexual.'

'How disgusting! I had no idea.'

'Really? You rented a flat to someone without seeing any identity document? What about the contract?'

'I—we hadn't got round to making a contract. It's something I've been meaning to see to . . . You know how these things are . . .' There was no aggression in the voice now.

'How long?'

'She—it must be almost two years.'

'And you hadn't got round to making a contract.'

'It started off on a more or less friendly basis and I suppose we just never got round to it.'

'I see. How much did this friendly arrangement cost Luigi Esposito per month?'

'Really, I couldn't say without checking. I never think about money—'

'If you'd like to check I have plenty of time.'

'Let's say half a million, plus condominium expenses, of course.'

'Of course. You have the receipts?'

'Receipts. No, you see—'

'It was a friendly arrangement. Yes, you said so. I imagine —this being a friendly arrangement—he agreed not to register his residence here at the town hall?'

'That's really none of my business. I had no idea—and no idea of its not being a woman, either, I assure you. When you only see someone passing occasionally on the stairs I doubt if we so much as said good morning to each other more than once in all the two years.'

'But you had this friendly arrangement.' It was common enough anyway, no contract, no receipts, no rent control, no taxes, but the Lulu's in the case, socially unacceptable and with money to spare, were perfect victims for such exploitation. He was convinced that Lulu had been paying rent in millions rather than hundreds to this highly respectable landlady but he also knew that he would never be able to prove it. And if she 'didn't know' that Lulu was a transsexual, it went without saying that she would never have seen any clients going in or out. He saw her eyes wavering under his stare but he knew her sort. He was wasting his time. So all he said was, 'We'll need to keep the keys. The Public Prosecutor's office will send someone to seal the entrance until further notice. Good evening, Signora.'

She watched him go without a word and he heard the

door close quietly behind him as he stumped down the stairs.

'I've found some good photographs,' Ferrini announced as he saw the Marshal come in. The photographs were spread out on the bed. The television was still on but the tape, thank God, had run out.

'Look at this one in the bathing suit. You have to admit he was better-looking than the real thing. Look at the thighs! And as for those eleven and a half ounces . . .'

The Marshal didn't look. He went straight to the bathroom. The young technician was shutting his case.

'I've finished if you want to look round.'

The Marshal said nothing, only gazed about him with troubled eyes. But as the young man started to push past him and leave he got hold of his arm.

'The sink.'

'What about it? It's clean as a whistle.'

'Pull it out.'

'What?'

'Pull it away from the wall.'

'Well . . . If you think . . .'

'Pull it out.'

'All right—but shouldn't we warn the owner?'

'No.'

They weren't equipped for a plumbing job but two of them managed to shift it, not very far but enough.

'Ferrini!' The Marshal called him without budging from his place just inside the door.

'Well, well, well!' said Ferrini. 'Good for you!'

The technicians homed in on the spot, delighted and not at all resentful. 'You learn a new one every day!'

The Marshal still didn't budge. He didn't say anything, either, only stared at the strip of tile that had been behind the sink. It was patterned with vertical trickles of red.

CHAPTER 5

When they got outside a fine drizzle was falling in the dark street which looked oily in the yellow lamplight.

The Marshal said, 'We should pick up anybody who said they knew Esposito had gone to Spain. You've got them listed from the other night?'

'There were only a couple, Mimi and Peppina. He didn't seem to have many friends.'

'As long as you know who they are and where to find them . . .'

To him the other night was no more than a blur, the doll-like faces all the same, the names meaningless. Titi, Lulu, Mimi . . .

'You want to pick them up tonight?'

'Tonight, yes.'

Ferrini peered at his watch in the gloom. 'It's early yet. There'll be nobody there until going on midnight. We might just catch a restaurant still open, what do you think?'

'No . . . no, I think I'll go home if you don't mind.'

'All right by me.'

'My wife will be wondering . . .'

'Ah. Mine expects me when she sees me.'

'I'll pick you up at Borgo Ognissanti.'

Whether or not Teresa would be wondering, the fact was he wanted to go home for the sake of being somewhere normal and familiar, to take the taste away . . .

It was Bruno who greeted him in the first place, not Teresa. He must have heard the car on the gravel and was hovering near the door.

'There's this urgent message, Marshal, at least . . .'

'What is it? We'd better go into my office.'

'I promised to tell you as soon as you came in, so—'

'All right.' He switched on the light and unbuttoned his damp overcoat. 'What is it?'

'This boy came looking for you. He'd been to Borgo Ognissanti and they'd sent him here because of your being in charge of the case—the pre-packed—'

'Don't you start calling it that, too.'

'Sorry, sir.'

'And don't call me sir.'

'Sorry, Marshal—only with not knowing the victim's name . . .'

'Esposito.'

'You found out?'

'Today. Who's this boy?'

'One of the ones we picked up the other night, or so he says, I mean he looks like a he and was dressed ordinarily, little thin kid.'

'I remember. Well? What did he want?'

'He seemed to be scared out of his wits for a start. I suppose it's no wonder, is it, now it's in all the papers about the pre—about this murder. Anyway, it seems that all the people who were picked up were told not to leave Florence without permission and what it amounts to is that he's too scared to go out at night and—and work, and he has to, to live, I mean, so he wants to leave. He says if you let him go to Milan he'll report his address, not disappear or any-thing—'

'No, no, no.'

'I suppose not. Can't blame him for being scared. I bet they all are. The thing is, he says he's not really one of them so it's nothing to do with him. He said he told them that the other night. I think he thought that because he knew you you'd make an exception and—'

'He doesn't know me. I saw him for five minutes when they brought him in. Listen, I'm tired—'

'But, Marshal, I wouldn't have—I mean, I'd have sent him away without bothering you but he does know you. He said he used to live near you down in Sicily and that your wife knows his mother.'

'I see. Is his name Luciano?'

'That's right. Enrico. You do know him, then?'

'I didn't recognize him. I haven't seen him since he was nine or ten.'

'That explains it, because he didn't recognize you either, perhaps because you weren't in uniform, but when he went to Borgo Ognissanti today and they said that you—'

'All right. I can't do anything about it now. I'll see tomorrow. But if he goes anywhere it won't be to Milan. He can go home to his mother who's looking for him.'

'Did I do wrong, telling you?' Bruno's face was apprehensive.

'No, no. Don't worry about it.'

He left Bruno to switch out the lights and lock up and went through to his own quarters. He'd never had any time for the Luciano woman, but even so, to have to tell her that her son . . . Teresa might . . . but no, he couldn't even see himself telling Teresa.

'You haven't eaten, have you?' She was waiting for him in the kitchen, preparing something, perhaps for the next day.

'No.'

'Sit down, then. I fed the boys but I thought I'd wait for you. It's miserable eating alone.'

Not that it turned out to be a cheery event eating together. He ate slowly, staring at his plate and never saying a word. Teresa looked at him, as apprehensive as Bruno had been. He was never a great talker but for him to be like this there had to be something really wrong.

More to provoke him into speaking than to know the answer she said, 'Did I do wrong to wait for you? You look as if you want to be on your own.'

There was no telling whether the question had penetrated.

He chewed thoughtfully, staring past her, and then said, 'There's something still cooking.'

She looked round. 'What? Oh, that. It's a sauce for tomorrow. I thought I'd make lasagne for lunch.'

'Tomorrow? Why?'

'It's Sunday.'

'Oh.' But then it appeared that her question had sunk in because after a moment he added, 'There's not much point in waiting for me, not while this business is going on.'

It was the first time he had so much as mentioned 'this business'. She knew all about it, of course, having taken a cake up to the boys' kitchen and got it all out of young Bruno. After that she'd followed it up in the papers and read the Prosecutor's comments. She made no attempt to question her husband now, knowing it was the sort of thing that embarrassed him, but still she was convinced that there was something in particular bothering him. Well, if he wouldn't say, he wouldn't, besides which, she had more important things on her mind. That was the real reason why she'd waited to eat alone with him and why she had to get his attention. Lasagne made as good an opening as any other.

'I've got a nice roast as well and I thought in the afternoon . . . of course you might be busy. Salva?'

'Mm.'

'I can see you've got a lot on your mind but I have to talk to you. I'm so worried about that boy. He can't go on—'

'Who told you?'

'Told me?'

'About the boy. Was it Bruno?' He was annoyed but relieved as well. After all, if she knew then perhaps she'd be willing to tell the mother. 'It's a bad business. A boy of that age and no future in front of him. No future at all. Bruno had no business . . . Still, what's done is done and you had to know sometime.'

Teresa had no idea what he was talking about but was wise enough to keep quiet and let him get whatever it was off his chest. She'd catch on soon enough if he kept talking. She poured him a drop of wine. He kept talking.

'Whatever you say, I blame the mother. He had no childhood. Out on the streets at eleven at night selling contraband cigarettes and already in the hands of the police at what age? Nine? Ten?'

'Ten.' She was with him now. But what on earth had the boy done? Surely he couldn't be involved in 'this business'?

'Why do people have children in this day and age if they don't want them? And if they have them they should be made to be responsible for them! If it wasn't for Ferrini being the man he is he'd have put him inside the other night but he could see there was no point. He won't live long as it is, that was Ferrini's opinion and he's right. It's the parents who should be inside. How can anyone neglect a child to that extent? And now I'm the one who has to tell her that her son's walking the streets of Florence dressed up like a dog's dinner, his face plastered with make-up—and then I've no doubt she'll start wailing and calling on the Madonna!'

Teresa was still silent but now it was from shock. She put her own problem aside. It would keep until tomorrow. The world was full of people so much worse off than yourself. Make-up . . . little Enrico . . . She'd seen them, of course. They were on the streets at lunch-time, not only at night, so you couldn't avoid seeing them, but . . . *Enrico*!

'Well, she'll have to be told.' He got up from the table. Anger had got the better of embarrassment. He would talk to the woman himself.

'Salva! Are you sure . . .?'

But he was in the hall and shouting, 'Where's the number?'

'On the pad—but are you sure you should . . .' She gave it up, hearing him dial. She stood up herself and started moving plates about noisily, too agitated to want to hear how he broke the news. Despite her efforts a few words came through, enough to tell her that if his voice had been gruff with anger at the beginning of the conversation it was lowered in dismay by the end. He didn't come back in immediately and when he did he was wearing civilian clothing and tucking a scarf into his overcoat.

'I'll be late. Don't wait up.' His face was very pale.

Ferrini got back in the parked car. Its engine was running.

'Might as well leave it switched on. No point in freezing to death.'

'No.' The Marshal was hunched in the front passenger seat, his head sunk into his upturned collar as though he were indeed freezing.

'Mimi saw him go off in a car with a client about ten minutes ago. Bit of a nuisance but it's not the end of the world. He'll be back. Mimi's own alibi's as sound as a bell. Came out of the clinic himself the day Lulu was expected. That's how he knew.'

'Yes.' He stared out along the dark avenue where the globular white lights were blurred by raindrops.

Ferrini flicked a switch and cleared the windscreen. Another black car was parked in front of their own. Each time a crawling vehicle with its solitary prowler went by the Marshal saw the silhouette of Bruno conversing earnestly with the man Ferrini had brought along. Then the headlights would sweep on their way and the silhouettes dissolve into trickling blackness. Ferrini flicked the wipers on again. Much further along the avenue a pale figure stepped out from the shelter of the trees, bent towards a car window and almost at once straightened up and retreated from sight.

'Filthy night,' commented Ferrini, to fill the silence.

'Yes.'

'But business as usual. What a way to make a living. Out half naked on a night like this. Makes you think.'

'Yes.'

'You got something on your mind?'

'No, no . . .'

'You're surely not still brooding about that kid? There are hundreds like him.'

'Yes. I wasn't . . . It's the mother. I'd never have expected—'

'What else could you expect? If things had been any different the kid wouldn't be what he is.'

'No. You're right, of course.'

And he was right. You only had to stop and think for a minute to realize that. Only, he hadn't stopped to think. He'd picked up the phone full of self-righteous anger which was soon doused by the woman's cold fury. There'd been only a quick intake of breath followed by a second or so of silence after his announcement. Then the spitting abuse.

'The little bastard! That sodding little—he's coining it in! That's why he thinks fit to keep clear of his family! He's coining it in and don't tell me otherwise because I know what they make here, never mind a place like Florence. And the little shit hasn't coughed up so much as a penny to his mother. Well, am I his mother or am I not? It's unnatural! Jesus, Mary and Joseph, the thanks you get for bringing kids into the world! If I had my time over again . . .'

'The worst of it is, it's probably true . . .'

'What's that?'

'That the boy's been hiding what he was doing so that she wouldn't get at his money, not because he was ashamed.'

'Likely enough. Didn't you say his mother was a prostitute? I doubt if he feels he was destined for a finer life.'

The Marshal hunched deeper into his overcoat in silence and they waited.

It wasn't a long wait. A quarter of an hour at the most and then a white car pulled over on the opposite side of the avenue, slowing just enough to let the fur-clad passenger out and swinging out and away at speed.

It might have gone very differently if it hadn't been for the other client who must have been parked somewhere behind them out of sight. He, too, had been waiting for Peppina and the minute the white car pulled away he slid forward, obscuring Peppina from their view. If he hadn't done that, if they hadn't been afraid of his being whisked away from them again, they wouldn't all four have jumped from their cars and started running across the road and Ferrini wouldn't have thought it necessary to shout.

The client panicked first, roaring away in a cloud of exhaust fumes and winging one of the crawling cars that he overtook with his passenger door which was swinging open. Peppina hesitated but not for long. By the time they reached the other side of the road he was fleeing between the trees with his fur coat swinging out behind him and Bruno and his mate on his heels. The Marshal, past all that sort of thing and always too heavy to be much of a runner, stood still on the grass verge. Ferrini plunged forward and followed the others. He was younger and thinner than the Marshal but he was surely impelled more by enthusiasm than serious intent. However that was, the Marshal was left alone. The little episode, over almost before it began, seemed to have had no effect on business. The man whose car had been winged leaned out to swear and make a rude gesture but nobody else gave any sign of having noticed anything.

The Marshal peered through the drizzly blackness but could make out nothing. Beyond the trees, if he remembered rightly, there was another, narrower road with a cycle path running on the other side of it. Then a grassy bank dropping steeply down to the river. But nothing was visible beyond the trees immediately in front of him. He felt his way forward cautiously, holding one hand up near his face to protect it from invisible branches. At first he could hear only the slowly turning car engines on the avenue behind him, the occasional hoot of a horn. Of the chase no sound reached him. As he left the avenue further behind he began to be conscious of the sound of his own soft footfall in the wet grass and of his slow breathing. The rain drizzled in silence, enveloping him in wetness like a black mist. He started to wonder if he should have stayed where he was in case their quarry turned back to make for the road, but it was too late now since he wasn't at all sure where he was. He felt about him. He seemed to be in some sort of clearing. Something scurried away from his feet, perhaps a rat or a squirrel, disturbed by his passage. Then he heard a shout. That was surely Bruno's voice. No answering shout came, only another long silence. He really wished now that he'd stayed where he was—or at least, if he had to go bumbling around in the dark he might have thought to get a torch from the car. It had all happened too quickly for him. He stuffed his big hands in his pockets and stood as still as the trees around him, thankful, as usual, that Ferrini was there. At least he knew who it was they were chasing. Somebody by the name of Peppina, he'd said. One of the ones they'd picked up the other night, but the Marshal couldn't for the life of him put a face to the name.

'Did you notice their faces?' Ferrini had said. But he hadn't noticed anything except that they all looked alike to him. What was he doing in charge of a case like this? Not that that was his fault. Even so, it was all wrong. He was out of his depth and the best thing he could do was to go to the Captain as soon as possible and tell him so. It was hardly even fair to Ferrini that he should have to work with someone so incompetent so that he had to do everything himself. Ferrini had said he was impressed by that business of the sink, but what would he have thought if he knew the truth? That when Teresa had first moved up here from Syracuse and started smartening up his quarters she'd nagged him for months to plaster up the tiny space between the sink and the wall in the bathroom. He'd never got round to it and she'd had to get somebody in to do it in the end. She said the dirty water trickled down behind and bred

germs. He couldn't for shame tell Ferrini that. The whole
thing was ridiculous; he wasn't a detective, he wasn't trained
for it and it wasn't his job. The Station at Pitti was a quiet
spot where he was expected to keep order in his district,
settle the odd dispute between neighbours, send in reports
from tourists who'd had their bags stolen, organize security
for the big exhibitions in the galleries at the Palace. So what
the devil was he doing in the park at one in the morning
getting his feet wet to no good purpose?

The pale figure of Peppina crashed into the clearing with
such suddenness that he had no time to move. He was so
still as to be invisible and the running figure hit him full
square, almost knocking the breath out of his body. The
Marshal made a hesitant grab and then backed off as his face
was attacked. His hesitation was caused by his confusion as
to what he was fighting against. Peppina was almost naked,
the fur coat having got lost during the chase. A woman's
breasts were pressing against his thick coat, a woman's nails
had gouged the skin near his eyes, but a man's hand began
closing round his throat and a man's muscles were proving
as strong if not stronger than his own. He started fighting
the man but he had left it late and his hesitation might have
been the death of him if Bruno hadn't leaped forward and
torn Peppina away.

'Good lad!' came Ferrini's voice and the other two approached. Of course Ferrini had a torch. He shone it down
on the writhing white figure. Bruno was astride the prostrate
Peppina, struggling to get the hands behind the back and
handcuff them. The others helped and Peppina was soon
dragged upright and taken off to the parked cars.

The Marshal had recognized the face by this time. Peppina was the one who'd turned on him that night in the
office: '*Is looking enough or do you want to touch?*'

Now he sat in the front of the car, conscious of his smarting
face and of the strong perfume still clinging to the front of
his overcoat. Peppina was in the back, handcuffed now to

Bruno. Ferrini's lad was following in the other car. Peppina had made row enough for ten at first until she saw what Ferrini was holding on his knee.

'You threw your handbag away in the bushes when you were running off,' Ferrini said. 'I'm sure you wouldn't do a thing like that except by mistake, so I picked it up for you.'

And Peppina fell silent.

As they drove out of the park towards the yellow lighting on Ponte alla Vittoria, Ferrini slowed down.

'Did you want a word with Carla? You said you'd ask him about identifying . . .'

'He's here?'

'Over there, by the hotel. Do you want me to stop?'

Carla stood very still and upright. Long legs in white fishnet tights, a scrap of something lacey that didn't quite reach up to the high breasts. One hand was placed on the left hip, the other hanging loose but motionless. The long white fur was pushed back from the shoulders and hung down behind almost to the feet. There was something different from the figures in the park that swung forwards from their huddled stance under the sheltering trees. There was no sign of life, no flicker of response to the dark falling rain, to the headlights that swept slowly over the still, white figure and passed on. They came close enough to stop and speak but the Marshal, unable to recognize even at that distance, the person he had talked to in a tidy little flat, hesitated and then said, 'Drive on.' It was the eyes. They had stared past him, past the cars streaming across the bridge, past the river and the floodlit palaces on the other bank, past everything. The blank and sightless eyes of a statue.

'What time did you arrive at Lulu's flat?'

'I told you.'

'And I don't believe you.'

'It couldn't have been before midnight. I never go out before half past eleven.'

'You went out before that. You went out to eat at Lulu's flat.'

'That's a lie. I ate at the trattoria where I always eat.'

'Who with?'

'I can't remember . . .' Peppina was rubbing at his blackened fingers with a handkerchief but the fingerprinting ink only spread a little and didn't come off. He was nearly naked but the Marshal's overcoat was pulled around his shoulders. Ferrini had laughed at him but he had refused to have Peppina brought in uncovered. It had been Bruno who had inadvertently divested him of the fur coat when trying to grab him during the chase and now it was lying in a sodden heap somewhere in the park.

Ferrini's interrogation wasn't vicious, only insistent. He was too sure of his ground to have recourse to anger. No matter what Peppina might admit or deny, there was no getting away from the evidence lying on the desk between them. His handbag had contained, among other things, a packet of traveller's cheques in the name of Luigi Esposito.

'What about the money? There must have been some cash as well as these. Have you spent it?'

'There was no money. I never saw any money.'

'We've already fingerprinted the flat.'

'I never said I wasn't at the flat.'

'And the handbag.'

'I never touched her handbag. She'd gone when I got to the flat. I swear that's true. I saw her the night before. She said she was leaving soon. When I went to the flat that night she'd gone.'

'He hadn't gone. He was dead. He died right after a meal, the meal we found on the table, the meal you shared with him.'

'That's a lie! I told you, I ate at the trattoria! You can

check—and then I went to work at my usual place. I only went to Lulu's flat after that and she'd gone!'

'So how did you get in? Well? Come on, let's hear it. You went to the flat at midnight and Lulu wasn't there so how did you get in?'

'I want a lawyer! I'm not answering any more questions.'

'Please yourself. With or without your lawyer you'll talk to the Prosecutor tomorrow morning and I hope you'll have a better story ready because this one stinks. Take him away.'

When he'd been removed, Ferrini and the Marshal looked at each other and then at the traveller's cheques.

'He might think better of it overnight,' Ferrini said, 'and then our troubles really start.'

'How do you mean?'

'We can keep him in a cell here for a day or two but once he's charged we'll have to move him to prison. The men's prison won't want him and the women's prison will refuse to take him. In the meantime I'd say enough's enough for one night, what about you?' He slid the traveller's cheques into an envelope and locked them away. Then he tipped the rest of Peppina's stuff back into the handbag. As well as make-up and various crumpled bits of paper, there were cigarettes and a bottle of pills.

'Do you think he did it?' the Marshal asked.

'Why? Don't you? He could have this stuff back, I suppose . . .'

'I'll see to it. Then, as you say, enough's enough . . .'

It was difficult to hear anything down in the basement because of the noise from the generator right in front of the two cells. It was unbearably hot. The Marshal had himself let into the cell on the left and offered the handbag to Peppina who was curled up on the worn brown blanket covering the hard narrow bed. He sat up and snatched at it, clutching at once at the cigarettes and lighting one with trembling hands.

'Thanks.' He threw the packet down on the blanket and

fished anxiously for the bottle of pills. 'Thank God for that. I can't sleep without them, can't sleep a wink . . . oh shit!' He crumpled up with his head on his knees. His sobs were dry, sobs of fear. 'Oh shit . . . what a thing to happen to me. And all because of that bitch Lulu.'

'Did you hate him?'

'Lulu? Everybody hated her! Everybody!' He looked up, pushing back his long fair hair with the lethal red fingernails whose effects the Marshal could still feel. 'Listen, I swear to God I never killed her—besides it must have been a maniac, chopping somebody up like that, it makes me shudder to think! I've never harmed a fly, never. I've never been in prison either and I don't even take drugs. There's nothing against me and now this has to happen just when I wanted to get out!'

'Get out?'

'Out of this whole business. I've had enough. I never wanted to be a prostitute—what kind of life do you think it is? I'd decided to get out, start a little business on my own —well, nobody would give me a job, I know that—and now what will happen to me? I've had it. I know I've had it. Nobody will believe me, will they, because of what I am? I'll be convicted because of what I am even though I never touched her. I never even saw her. That bitch!'

'What was it about Lulu,' the Marshal asked, 'that everybody hated him?'

'She had so much money. They'd pay anything to have her. She didn't need to be on the streets, do you know that? With all the regulars she had and what they paid her she could have stayed at home, but she didn't. It wasn't enough that she had more than anybody, she had to snatch everybody else's clients as well, just for spite. Do you know what she'd do? She'd come out and sell herself at half the normal price just to take business off us! Can you believe that?'

'Had he no friends at all?'

'You're joking! All she cared about was herself and her

body. She spent a fortune on herself. Nobody could touch her for looks. You have to admit she was beautiful but she was rotten all through. A rotten stinking bitch! And because of her my life's ruined and over!' He gulped down two capsules and dropped the bottle on the floor as he flopped over face down on the bed. The black silk stockings he wore were torn and laddered and the half bare buttocks were caked with mud. It was too hot in the tiny cell but, more for decency's sake than anything, the Marshal adjusted his now dirty overcoat over the prostrate body and left.

Bruno was waiting in the car at the main entrance. He started up the engine but the Marshal said, 'I wouldn't mind walking. I feel like a bit of air.'

'But it's still raining, Marshal, and you've forgotten to get your overcoat back.'

'All right.' And he got into the car obediently.

Perhaps he'd got used to working such odd hours. At any rate he slept soundly through the morning until Teresa's efforts not to make a noise in the kitchen finally woke him. He lay there for a while, feeling heavy and warm, enjoying the peaceful atmosphere of Sunday, the smell of the roast just filtering through the closed door, the muffled voices of his family. He closed his eyes again for a few minutes and almost fell asleep, but then the insistent clamour of the bells of San Felice started up, followed closely by the more solemn and measured bell of the cathedral across the river. The minute he turned to look at the clock his face began to sting and the memory of last night flooded in to fill up his mind and destroy his moment of peace.

'Are you awake?' Teresa peeped round the door.

'Just about. There's a good smell.'

'It won't be ready for an hour yet. Shall I make you some coffee?' Her eyes were fixed on his smarting cheek. He'd poured iodine into the scratches before going to bed and it must have looked a sight but she went away without mentioning it.

He had a long shower and put on comfortable Sunday clothes, trying to recapture the normal peaceful feeling he had woken up with. It was no use. The image of the torn and muddy figure lying on a threadbare brown blanket intruded. What sort of a Sunday was he having in the tiny hot cell with the noise of the generator thundering for hours on end?

During lunch, the boys kept glancing at his face but they had obviously been told not to mention it. All three of them were ostentatiously not mentioning it. He was hungry and ate a lot without saying much.

When the boys were about to leave the table, Giovanni hesitated.

'Mum, have you—'

'Later. Go and study for an hour, both of you. Your dad's tired.'

'He's only just got up,' Totò objected.

'Do as I say.'

They went to their room.

'What's Giovanni want?'

'Nothing. Have five minutes while I clear away. Do you want the paper?'

'No. No, I'd rather be doing something. What about a stroll through the Boboli Gardens? The weather seems to be clearing up.' A sharp mountain wind was driving away the ragged remains of last night's cloud. It would be colder but brighter and more cheerful.

'Well . . .'

'Or we could walk into the centre,' he conceded, 'if you fancy looking at the shop windows.'

'It's not that. I don't mind, only I'd promised the boys . . .'

'Promised them what?'

'That we'd take them down to the Cascine with their bikes.'

'No.'

'But, Salva, you know they never get a chance to ride them. You don't want them to go on the road—'

'How can they possibly go on the roads with the traffic there is in this city? It's out of the question!'

'I know it is. That's why I promised to take them down to the park. I can't let them go on their own because the roads around the Ponte alla Vittoria are so dangerous.'

'Go on their own? Traffic or no traffic, they do not go in that park on their own!'

'What are you so angry about? We've taken them before. It's a nice walk for us and they can ride up and down to their hearts' content on the cycle paths. They need some fresh air. Well, never mind, I'll take them myself. Perhaps you should go back to bed . . .'

One of her unfinished sentences meaning 'Perhaps you should go back to bed if you're so tired as to be in such a bad temper.' She started clearing the table rapidly.

Although he didn't want to read it, he took the newspaper for camouflage and sat himself in the living-room, staring at the front page without reading a word. Within half an hour the three of them presented themselves, Teresa in a fur coat, the boys in anoraks with scarves tied tightly at their necks.

'We're off,' she said.

He got up.

'Are you going to have a nap?'

He got his coat on. 'Where are my sheepskin gloves?'

'In the drawer where they always are.'

'Hmph.'

'Put a scarf on, there's a cold wind.'

And they all set off.

Despite the cold wind, there were plenty of people in the park. The roundabout was going near the entrance and in the first little piazza there was a van selling slices from a whole roast pig on chunky sandwiches. They joined the families strolling down the pedestrian road running by the

river and the boys took off at speed, racing each other along
the cycle path. The smallest children on tricycles, plastic
horses and pedal cars wound slowly in and out among the
groups of strolling adults, calling to each other and their
parents for attention. On the benches set along the road sat
escaped husbands listening in peace to the football match,
their little radios glued to their ears, their collars turned up
against the wind.

'Are you feeling better?' Teresa asked, linking her arm
through his.

'I'm all right.' After all, it was a different world here on
a bright and windy Sunday afternoon. So far away from the
world of last night. And yet his glance sometimes strayed
to the right where untended brush grew in a tangle below
the trees. Somewhere in there lay Peppina's sodden fur,
if someone hadn't already found and made off with it.
He wasn't sure where it had all happened, having
bumbled around so much in the dark. A bit further down,
maybe . . .

'They ought to do something about all that mess. Just
look at it.' Teresa was pointing in the opposite direction, to
the far bank of the river where the Arno in flood had left its
detritus dangling from the branches of trees overhanging
the water. 'All those plastic bags and all that filthy rubbish
just left there. It could be so nice along here.'

The boys came racing back, Totò well in the lead, his
face red and his eyes glittering as he pedalled furiously. He
always overdid everything.

'Mum! Can we go as far as the Indian?'

'If you like—don't shout so much and slow down or you'll
exhaust yourself.' But he was off again, almost crashing into
Giovanni who had started to turn round slowly. 'Race you
to the Indian and back!' They were soon out of sight.

The two of them walked on at the same sedate pace as
everyone else, pursued by the football commentary that
occasionally broke into a roar of excitement or dismay.

'We may as well walk as far as the Indian ourselves,' Teresa suggested.

'If you like.'

But they hadn't got there before a woman a little way in front of them gave an irritated shout and just managed to dodge Totò's bicycle as the boys came racing back along the tarmac.

'Beat you!' yelled Totò. 'That's twice I've beaten you!'

'Totò' cried both his parents together. 'What are you trying to do, kill somebody? Get back on the cycle path. What do you think it's there for?'

'But, Dad, you can't go as fast as on the tarmac, it's too cindery!'

'Can't you see there are people walking here, small children, too? Now do as you're told.'

'But everybody else goes on the tarmac! There's nobody on that stupid cycle path except for us. It's so slow, it's all cindery. Everybody else—'

'Do as your father tells you,' interrupted Teresa, 'or we go straight home.'

Giovanni was already pushing his bike back through a gap in the low hedge. Totò got off and followed him, but when Giovanni mounted again and pedalled on, he carried on pushing his bike with exaggerated slowness to show how bad the path was, his reddened face sullen. He was the last to arrive in the circular piazza, where he went on pushing his bike in wide circles around the baldaquin-like monument sheltering the bust of a dead Indian prince.

It was Teresa who suggested they sit down for a moment. As they settled on a bench she watched Totò unhappily.

'I'm worried about him, Salva.'

'He'll be all right. He's just sulking.'

'It's not that. I've been worried for a while now. I wanted to tell you last night but . . . I don't know whether we did the right thing, following the teacher's advice. Keeping him in all the time, I mean.'

Giovanni was riding round in figures of eight. When Totò pushed by him he said, 'Why don't you get on your bike?'

'I don't feel like it.' His face was still red and angry.

'They've never quarrelled so much as they have in this last few weeks. Giovanni and his friend like to do their homework together in the boys' room and they don't want him. There's a scene nearly every afternoon. I don't know what you think, but my feeling is we've tried what she suggested and it's only made him worse. I can force him to stay in but I can't force him to study. He pretends to, but he's just messing about. He only got five in Italian last week —and besides, he's unhappy, you can see that. Maybe if we let him play out in the afternoons—'

'No.'

'Just for an hour to see if—'

'No,' he repeated, staring not at the child but at the sluggish brown river flowing past, 'keep him at home where he's safe.'

CHAPTER 6

Captain Maestrangelo put his head round the door just in time to see the Marshal coming along the corridor.

'Ah. I was about to send someone to look for you. I have to go out shortly. Come in.'

The Marshal obeyed.

'Take a seat. I got your message first thing this morning —I imagine you've been pretty busy since then. I saw the Prosecutor just now as he was leaving. He was very complimentary about you.'

'Me?'

'Certainly. You've seen the files of the other cases of this sort. Nobody was hopeful about clearing this one up at all, let alone in a matter of days.'

'Ah . . .' Why had he gone and made this appointment first thing? He should have waited, at least until after this morning's interrogation . . . He pulled himself together and said, 'The credit should go to Ferrini. I'd have been lost without him. He found Peppina.'

'Peppina? Is that . . .'

'Giuseppe Bianco. He calls himself Peppina.'

Thank God somebody had found him an old track suit to wear for his interview with the Prosecutor. The lawyer had done all the talking, Peppina neither confirming nor denying without looking at him first. He had been trembling the whole time and on the verge of tears. The Prosecutor had regarded him throughout with undisguised disgust. The Captain was wearing a similar experssion now as he said, 'It seems he has a different story this morning from the one he told when you arrested him last night.'

'Not altogether. He never denied having gone to the flat, only he said the victim wasn't there, in which case he couldn't have got in without breaking in and there were no signs of anybody having done that.'

'So now he's dreamed up an accomplice with keys.'

'It could be true.'

'The Prosecutor thinks not.'

'I know.'

'You don't agree? Surely it's the first thing he would have told you had it been true?'

'I don't know.'

'But surely, a nameless, faceless client we've no hope of finding and checking on. It sounds to me like pure invention. A last-ditch attempt to sow a seed of doubt despite the evidence of those traveller's cheques. It'll do him no good, I rather think. Some of these lawyers are too clever for their own good.'

'Yes . . . but he's not faceless or even entirely nameless . . .'

'What? You mean this mythical client?'

'They call him Nanny. I don't know why. I've seen a photo of him.'

The Captain regarded the troubled face before him for a moment without speaking. There was never any way of knowing what was going through the fellow's mind and even if you asked him it was a waste of time. The Captain knew this of old. The Marshal was none too bright and far from articulate but there was no getting away from the fact that he didn't miss much and that the quieter he got, the nearer he was to whatever he was after. If he'd been capable of explaining just what it was he was after it would have been possible to help him, but he wasn't. Some people laughed at Guarnaccia, and it was true that he was slow and had a tendency to bumble about in an absent-minded way and to stare at you without answering because he hadn't followed what you'd said. It was a lucky thing that he'd got into the Prosecutor's good books, but he wouldn't stay there long if he tried going off on some track of his own the way he sometimes did.

'Don't get yourself in any trouble,' he advised.

'No, no . . .'

'It's not worth it.'

The Marshal stared at him in a way that made him add, 'I only mean . . . He probably is guilty, you know, in which case you'd be sticking your neck out for no good reason.'

'If he's guilty, yes.'

'You obviously think he's not. There are those traveller's cheques, remember. The Prosecutor told me he'd already forged the second signature.'

'Yes . . .'

'*You admit you signed these, copying Esposito's signature?*'

'*I . . . yes . . .*'

'*And you expected to be able to change them? Don't you know that they must be signed at the moment of exchange and proof of identity given?*'

'*Yes.*'

'*So what did you intend to do with them?*'

'*I . . . he . . .*'

'*My client has a customer, someone who works in a bank. He was to have taken the cheques that night which was why she—he had them in his bag.*'

'*Would that be the one who was in such a hurry to disappear when the carabinieri arrived?*'

'*Exactly.*'

That was a witness they would certainly never find. Funny that the lawyer should . . .

'What are you thinking?'

'Nothing,' the Marshal replied, 'I wasn't thinking anything. I just remembered that the lawyer accidentally referred to his client as "she".'

'Meaning?'

'Nothing. It just struck me . . .'

It really was impossible to help the man! Perhaps it was a mistake to give him the case. He'd never thought it would come to anything, that was the truth. He wondered if he should take him off it now—but how could he? Guarnaccia wasn't the sort to be unduly upset, but the Prosecutor would be furious. He was delighted with the way things had gone. There was nothing to be done except to give due warning . . . He'd already done that, but couldn't help saying it again.

'Be careful. It does nobody any good to annoy a prosecutor. You know the power they have.'

'Yes. I haven't said I disagree with him.'

'But you thought it.'

'I don't think anything. I'm just trying to understand . . .'

'But for goodness' sake, Guarnaccia! The chap attacked you when you were arresting him. Look at your face—and he even went for your throat from what I've heard. By all accounts he's a bit crazy or at the very least unbalanced.'

'Unbalanced, yes.' The hormones they took . . . Ferrini

had said. 'They go up in smoke at the least thing' or some such remark.

'And apparently he admits having hated Esposito.'

'A lot of people did. But not that much, I would have thought.'

'You can't be sure of that.'

'I'm not sure of anything . . . He went for me that first night we brought a bunch of them in—not physically, I don't mean . . . He flared up. He's the sort that flares up . . . Ferrini said—'

'Well then,' insisted the exasperated Captain, 'what more do you want? An unbalanced transsexual who hates another and is found in possession of the other's money after the murder. Of course you have doubts, it's only right at this stage. But you can't say that anybody's incapable of murder when pushed far enough. He may have more reason for hating his victim than he's saying.'

'That's true.' How could he explain when he didn't understand himself? He sat there looking at the Captain hopefully. He was an intelligent man. He ought to be able to explain what was wrong. The Captain leaned back in his chair and drummed with his fingers on the edge of the polished desk.

'Well, all I can say is—' the thing was useless but he'd done his best—'you'll be very unwise to make any move, however apparently legitimate, that will get you in trouble with the Prosecutor. Very unwise. And I can tell you from experience that he's not the worst of them, not by a long way. He knows his business better than most. I'm not saying you may not be right, only that you shouldn't stick your neck out, both for your own benefit and because this is not a case of petty theft we're talking about but an extremely nasty and cold-blooded killing such as I haven't come across in my whole career.'

'That's it.' The Marshal sat forward, his monosyllabic bulk suddenly animated. If only he had half the Captain's brains. 'That's exactly it. I couldn't put my finger on it myself.'

Then his eye fell on the Captain's watch and he looked at his own. 'It's half past ten. If you'd excuse me, sir, I have to be at the Medico-Legal Institute and I'm going to be late.'

'Of course. I'm going to be late myself; I was all but on my way when you came to see me.' They stood up and went their different ways.

It was only when the Captain stopped wondering what it was he was supposed to have put his finger on that he started wondering just what the devil Guarnaccia had come to see him for at all. It's doubtful whether the Marshal himself could have told him by this time, since he had quite forgotten that he wanted to be taken off the case.

'You understand that it's not going to be pleasant?'

'I should think that's putting it mildly. Just give me a minute to put some lipstick on. God, I look pale.' From the bedroom Carla's voice said, 'I'm not used to getting up so early, I look a sight.'

When he came back the Marshal said, 'That photograph, the one you showed me.'

'The one of Lulu?'

'That's right. Would you mind letting me have it? Just for a day or two?'

'You can keep it, for all I care—that's if I can remember where I put it. I don't know why I kept it anyway except that I always liked myself in that frock.' He started rummaging through a drawer. 'Hell, what did I do with it? Maybe in my bedroom . . .' From there he called, 'In any case Lulu must have had one. Didn't you come across one in her flat? I suppose you must have been there?'

'Yes. I don't remember . . .' He thought of the pile of photographs on the silk sheet and Ferrini . . . '*Look at those thighs, and as for the eleven and a half ounces . . .*' And he'd hardly glanced at them because of his embarrassment.

'There might have been a copy but I'm not sure, so I'd be grateful if you'd find yours.'

'I've found it. Here.' He brought it to him. 'Keep it.'

'Thanks.'

Carla, his coat round his shoulders, parked on the arm of a chair while he sat looking at it. The birds in their cage were huddled together sleepily on their perch. Perhaps they didn't chirp today because it was rather dark in the little sitting-room. The wind had dropped this morning and heavy clouds were gathering, ready for a thorough downpour.

'Are you going to publish it in the paper?'

'No . . . no, I don't think so—in any case, if that should happen I can cut you off it.'

He shrugged. 'I don't care. I've got nothing to hide.'

'No.'

'What about Peppina?'

'What about him.'

'You know what I mean. She's going to have a hard time, right? Even if she didn't do it, because of what she is.'

He could hardly deny it. Instead he asked, 'Is he a friend of yours?'

'Not particularly—to tell you the truth I tend to avoid her. She's so jumpy, quarrelsome. She makes me nervous. If you ask me she should change her doctor.'

'You think the hormone treatment . . .?'

'That's just my opinion. It could be just the way she is, but in any case, if I were her, I'd change my pills. Still, I don't suppose she'll ever get out now. She wasn't tough enough for this job. It was Mimi telephoned to say she'd been arrested last night and I said right away, "It would happen to her." I can tell sometimes with people, that they're no good at surviving, do you understand what I mean?'

'I think so.'

'Is there really much against her?'

'I'm afraid there is.' He was tempted to tell more than he ought. Carla knew so much more about all the people concerned than he could ever hope to know. 'He's trying to put together a sort of alibi. We phoned the trattoria where he says he had dinner that night but nobody can remember. He often ate there but nobody's prepared to swear he was there that night. The other thing is—' he indicated the photograph—'this man you call Nanny. He says they were together, that Nanny picked him up from the place in the park where he always stands and took him to Lulu's flat. Nanny, he says, had a key. Is that likely?'

'Could be. I wouldn't give anybody the keys to my flat, but Lulu was a nut-case and he was a regular client. I've heard he spent a lot of time at her flat, so it's possible. I think—this is only hearsay, do you understand?—that Lulu had plans for taking him on as her man. She used to tell people he was loaded and could keep her. I'm not saying it's true but if it was then maybe he did have a key.'

'So she intended to give up the game?'

'Lulu? You're joking! There are some of us who do what we do because, being what we are, we can't get any other job, and some who want to do it for the money we can make, but Lulu—you shouldn't speak ill of the dead, I know, but Lulu was a hundred per cent prostitute. She enjoyed it. She'd have sold herself for the price of a cup of coffee. She was rotten to the core and even if Peppina did do it I feel sorry for her. You can bet she had her reasons and she wasn't the only one, I can tell you that for nothing. Lulu was such a spiteful bitch she'd do somebody a bad turn just for the pleasure of it, even if she had nothing to gain.'

'Like taking Nanny off you?'

'If you like. She only did it to spite me. She thought she was pulling a fast one on me but I couldn't have cared less. I told you, I don't like his sort and she was welcome to him.'

'What about his other clients?'

'How do you mean?'

'Could there be some client he'd treated badly and who might have had it in for him?'

'Any number, I should think. One for sure.'

'Nanny, for instance?'

'No, I was thinking of somebody else—Wait, maybe that's somebody for me . . .' A car horn was hooting in the street below. Carla drew the white curtain aside and looked down. 'There's a taxi waiting for someone.'

'For me.' It was partly a reluctance to subject Carla to being seen taken away in a squad car, partly an equal but unacknowledged reluctance to be seen driving him in his own car, that had prompted him to arrive in a taxi. The meter must be ticking away but taxis had no dividing glass and taxi-drivers no compunction about joining in any conversation going.

'Don't worry,' he said, 'the taxi can wait. Tell me about this client.'

'I can't tell you much except that he was from Milan and drove down here fairly regularly. Maybe he was some sort of commercial traveller. I don't even know his name, of course, but Lulu did. She found it out.'

'How?'

'She stole his identity card while he was undressed. You can probably guess what she used it for.'

'Blackmail?'

'That's right. He had a wife and kids in Milan. God knows how much she tried to screw him for by threatening to turn up on his doorstep and tell all. Poor sod. They say he tried to strangle her and no wonder, but Lulu knew how to defend herself. Whoever did for her must have known that, don't you think? It said in the paper they knocked her out with sleeping pills first.'

'Yes. What happened in the end?'

'With that Milanese chap? I don't know, but I imagine

he must have paid up. What else could he have done? In any case he made himself scarce. It must be nearly a year ago by now and I've never seen him around since. I bet she ruined him. Hadn't we better go? God! I haven't fed the cat! Mishi! Mishi!'

The little cat appeared from the bedroom, yawning, as though she, too, were unaccustomed to getting up in the mornings. She followed Carla into the kitchen, her tail pointing upwards expectantly.

'It won't take me a minute!'

'Don't worry . . .' But he, too, followed Carla into the kitchen, standing just inside the doorway, watching him open the tin. The little cat made no fuss but seated herself near her dish in the corner and waited quietly.

'One thing's for sure,' Carla said, scraping the food out on to a saucer, 'she couldn't have pulled a trick like that on Peppina. Peppina's got no wife and kids.'

'What about his parents? Do they know?' After his experience with the Luciano woman he might have thought to ask instead 'Did they care?' but her reaction was something so alien to him that it hadn't really penetrated.

'She's an orphan.' Carla placed the saucer of food next to the plastic water dish and Mishi sniffed it cautiously. 'She grew up in an orphanage, I think. Mishi, you're a real pain in the neck with your food fads. You liked it last time I gave it you, now get on with it.'

Mishi started to nibble slowly round the edges of the food, careful not to dirty her whiskers.

'Let's leave while she's eating, then she won't try to escape.'

Carla double locked the door as they left. The Marshal gave him a sidelong glance as they started down the stairs. There was nothing to dismay him about Carla in street dress. A little on the opulent side for his taste perhaps, but on the whole the impression was of a well-dressed young woman rather unusually tall. Nevertheless, as they reached the ground floor, a middle-aged woman with a shopping-bag came out of a door on the left and pushed past them very deliberately to get out the front door first, giving them a black look over her shoulder. If the Marshal hadn't put his hand out in time the door would have slammed in their faces.

'That's her, the nasty bag. The one who complained about my Mishi, I told you. Christ, it's starting to rain and I've no umbrella. Shall I go back and get one?'

'There's no need. I'll bring you back in the taxi.'

They got in and the Marshal directed the driver to the Medico-Legal Institute. It was a longish drive to the hospital city in the suburbs. Carla looked out of the window at the rainy streets for some time before asking, 'What's Peppina's lawyer like?'

'He seems sharp enough.' The Captain, he recalled, had thought him too clever for his own good.

'I don't mean that, I mean what does he look like?'

'Look like? Well, I don't know . . . tallish, thick-set . . . I'm not much of a hand at describing people. Why?'

'Plenty of dark hair, greying at the temples?'

'Yes . . . I think so.'

'Good. He's one of her regular clients. It's nice that he hasn't dumped her. Some of them would.'

'I suppose so.' He had been right, then, to suspect it. When he'd let out that 'she' it had crossed his mind right away.

After a while, when they had struggled through the traffic in the centre and taken the road out to the hospitals, Carla said, 'I'm getting a bit nervous. I've never had to do anything like this before. I've never seen anybody dead, let alone . . . Will it bother you if I smoke a cigarette?'

'No, no, but . . .' The Marshal, already embarrassed by his having opened his mouth at all in the presence of the driver who must have thought he'd picked up a man and a woman and was now hearing two men's voices, indicated the No smoking sign.

'Oh, Elio doesn't mind if it's me, do you, Elio? I've got to identify a body and I'm getting cold feet. I want a smoke.'

'Carry on. You're not telling me it's Lulu you've got to—'

'That's right.'

'Rather you than me. The paper said he'd been chopped—'

'Talk about something else, will you?'

'You knew Lulu?' the Marshal asked.

'Knew him? Took him to work many a time, like I do Carla. But that Lulu was a rum sort. Nobody could stand Lulu, right, Carla?'

'Dead right.'

'I take most of them to and fro but Lulu was a right nut-case—you remember, Carla, that dirty trick he pulled on that fellow from Milan?'

'I've just been telling the Marshal about it.'

'Bound to get the chop sooner or later, that one.'

'Who told you about the client from Milan?' the Marshal asked him quickly.

'Who told me? He did. He always stayed at the Excelsior, which is right near my rank. I ran him down to the park many a time and it was always Lulu he was after. You have to admit, Lulu was a smasher, better-looking than any woman, but a bad lot. I remember him complaining one time—the Milanese chap—that Lulu had taken it into his head one night to charge three times the usual price. He was furious.'

'But he paid?'

'Oh, he paid all right. There was nobody could touch Lulu for—let's say—certain little extras. He complained plenty, though.' The taxi-driver laughed. 'Then Lulu really gave him something to complain about and he hasn't been seen since. I take a left here, is that right?'

'Yes. You don't know the chap's name, by any chance?'

'I do that. He once had to give me a cheque one night because our friend Lulu had cleaned him out of cash. Name's Rossini.'

'You have a long memory if that was a year ago.'

'More than a year. But I'd have to have a very short memory to forget that name since I'm called Elio Rossini myself! Well, here you are and the best of luck. Wouldn't fancy a sight of Lulu in his present state myself.'

The Medico-Legal Institute was an imposing building with a broad flight of steps leading up to it. As they climbed, heads ducked against the downpour, the Marshal could sense Carla's increasing fear. He kept hesitating and looking up at the great doors.

'It'll be over very quickly,' he assured him.

It was over quickly, and the Marshal did his best for Carla by keeping him back a moment to ensure that the attendant exposed only the side of the head that still had flesh on it and kept a covering over the saw marks at the neck. But even so, the shaved crown which had been very perfunctorily sewn back in place made Carla give a first recoil of shock, and the clouded eye was distorted by the flattened folds of dead yellow flesh around it.

He got him out of the place as fast as the formalities allowed and they were half way down the steps when he saw him sag forward.

'I feel sick—I think I'm going to faint.'

And he cursed himself then for his selfishness and pusillanimity in bringing him in a taxi when they could have got away at once in his own car.

'There's a bar across there,' he said, taking the arm Carla was holding across his stomach. 'I'll get you a glass of something strong while I call a taxi.' Why hadn't he even thought to let the other one wait? Cursing himself, he led him across to the bar. He sat in a chair with his head down and the Marshal placed a glass of cognac in front of him before starting to telephone. He had counted on there being plenty of taxis around the hospital area but this rain made it difficult and he was some time in finding one.

Carla was sitting in the same position, not having touched the drink.

'I'm afraid if I try to swallow anything I'll throw up.'

All the way back in the taxi he kept his head down and his eyes shut and at times the Marshal wasn't sure whether he was conscious or not. When they arrived, he paid the driver before getting out so as to be free to help Carla to his feet.

He thrust his handbag at the Marshal. 'The keys . . . I daren't open my eyes, everything's spinning.'

He found the keys and opened the street door, then took the stairs as fast as he could to get the flat door open for him. Carla pushed past him without a word, holding both hands to his mouth. He must have reached the bathroom only just in time. The Marshal heard an explosive retch and then a deep groan. Then a gurgle of running water. It was some minutes before he reappeared.

'I'm sorry.'

'There's no need to apologize. You did well to hold out so long.' He was lingering near the still open door, wondering if he was fit to be left.

'Mishi!'

'What . . .'

'Mishi! She'll have got out! Oh God . . . Mishi . . .'

'I didn't see her go out . . .'

'Mishi!'

They were both on the stairs when the street door opened and the woman they had encountered earlier came in with two bags of shopping.

They started running down the stairs, the Marshal in front.

'The door!' Carla shouted. 'Shut that door!' The woman only stood gaping up at them, half way in with the door still open. The little black cat, until that moment invisible, leapt from where it was crouching beneath the bottom stair and shot out into the street. The Marshal ran on down and reached the pavement just as the No. 36 bus passed, going downhill at speed. There was no squeal of brakes. The driver didn't even notice the swift dark little creature that was caught by his back wheel and flung up on to the pavement almost at the Marshal's feet.

Its front paws made feeble movements as though it were still running. A small amount of blood issued from one ear on to the pavement. Then the tiny movements subsided. Mishi was dead.

'Any better?'

'I'll be all right now. I'm sorry I got so hysterical.' He was lying curled on the sofa and the Marshal stood before him, a glass still in his hand. 'It's just that Mishi was . . . There were times when she was the only happy thing in my life. Sometimes it's awful to have to work yourself up to —to going out there and performing, leaving your own personality at home, dressing up for the show. Sometimes, when I feel a bit down and I'm out there . . . I can think: Mishi's at home curled up, waiting for me in another world. She keeps my real world alive for me while I'm . . . And now, what will I do? I can't go out tonight. I just can't.'

'You should stay at home and rest. You've had two nasty shocks. Isn't there anyone who could stay with you?'

'It's all right. I'll call my mother, but not yet.' Although he'd calmed down he was still crying. 'I'll wait a bit. If I call her in this state it'll only upset her. That sleeping pill will work in ten minutes or so and when I've slept I'll call her. Are you in a hurry?'

'No, no . . .'

'If you could just stay a few minutes until the pill works. I can't face being on my own yet. You're a good sort.'

'It's the least I can do after what I've put you through.'

'Once I've slept a bit and talked to my mother I'll get myself going again.'

The Marshal put the glass down near a silver bowl of fruit standing on a low table and perched on the arm of a chair.

'Your mother . . .' He still couldn't take in the Luciano woman's reaction. 'Your mother doesn't—you needn't tell me this if it bothers you, but how did your mother react . . . I mean the shock when she found out . . .'

'About my being a transsexual?' He dried his eyes and blew his nose. 'There was never any shock, they always knew I wasn't—you know—normal, if that's the word. Even when I was small people often took me for a girl, no matter how they dressed me. Oh, I'm not saying they weren't upset. A wealthy bourgeois family and me their only son. They took me to doctor after doctor but it wasn't as though they could blame me at that age, could they? I remember when I got to adolescence they took me to a specialist and I was given male hormone injections for a while but they made me so ill my mother couldn't go on with it. I think they took me to somebody else then, another specialist who talked to me for a long time. He was nice. I wasn't upset by it at all. Anyway the upshot was that he told my parents to leave me be, that there was nothing they could usefully do.'

'But . . . what you're doing now . . .'

'Being a prostitute, you mean? Well, I left home first, that was one thing. I'd finished studying and I knew I couldn't face getting a job that would force me to dress all my life as a man and lead a completely false existence. There was only one other possibility, wasn't there? Do you understand? Mind you, if I'd known then what I know now . . . the danger, the exhaustion. Even so, I'm not complaining. There are times when I'd give anything to stop, but when all's said and done, I've been able to earn my living and I've been able to be myself, a transsexual. I

think if I'd had to pretend to be a man I'd have ended up
in a lunatic asylum. But my parents, although they accept
me as I am, never mention that they know I'm a prostitute.
They shut their eyes to it and I can't blame them for that.
I'd be the last one to throw it in their faces. Parents are
weird though, aren't they? I remember when I decided to
get my breasts done. My mother came to see me afterwards
—I wanted her to come, I had to tell her. I even showed
them to her. I suppose that's the only time you could say
there was anything like a shock—I mean, she might have
taken it badly. But she didn't. It wasn't long after I'd left
home and I was living in a tiny bedsit with a hole in the
wall of a bathroom. It was a mess, I hadn't really learned
to look after things the way I do now. My mother hardly
looked at my breasts—she just kept looking around her,
saying, "How can you live like this after the way we brought
you up?" I could see her point, of course. I'd grown up in a
ten-bedroomed villa with two full-time servants. Poor thing,
she was just shocked by the poky room and the mess. She's
all right, my mother. I know I've been luckier than most.'

'Yes. I think you must have been.'

'One of these days I'll give it all up. Not yet, but one day
. . . I'm falling asleep . . . If only I could sleep for days and
days and days . . . one day, when I find some peace and
quiet . . .'

The Marshal stood up. Carla was asleep, his mouth a
little open. He picked up his hat and left quietly.

CHAPTER 7

'Salva! If that's you, answer it, will you? I'm heating some
oil, I can't leave it . . .'

He took his hat off and picked up the phone with one
hand, unbuttoning his greatcoat with the other.

'Yes?'

'Is that the Guarnaccia residence?'

'Yes. Guarnaccia speaking.'

'I've got your son here. Totò. His real name's Salvatore, isn't it?'

His stomach gave an emptying downward lurch that made him clutch at the fragile table for fear of falling. Not this . . . Dear God, anything, but not this. Think! He of all people should know what to say, what to ask for. A signed newspaper, a photograph, or was it . . .

'Can you hear me?'

'Yes . . .' But his mouth was so dry the word could hardly form itself. Why? Why him? They had no money, that must be obvious. A vendetta? Somebody they wanted out of prison? Why? He should be thinking fast, of road-blocks, of a tap on this telephone, of what? What should be done first? But all he could think as he clutched harder and harder at the receiver which was slipping through his sweating hand was Totò . . . Totò . . .

'Hello? Are you sure you can hear me?'

'Yes . . .'

'Hold the line. I'll put him on.'

A silence that lasted for ever, that he daren't interrupt. Then Totò's voice, weak and far away.

'Dad?'

'Totò! Are you all right?'

'Yes. Dad . . .' He started crying and then his voice dissolved and there was another silence.

'Totò!' There were only faint, incomprehensible noises.

'Who is it?' called Teresa from the kitchen. He couldn't answer. There were voices somewhere in the background. A lot of voices, then a bump and somebody picked up the receiver.

'Hello? Are you still there?' It was a different voice.

'Yes.'

'Your son's a bit upset, as you heard.'

'What do you want? What?'

'Just to inform you. You've been lucky up to now. Worse could have happened to him if he'd tried to get away. This is the manager speaking.'

'Manager . . . You're—the boss?'

'If you like. Anyway, we've decided to let the matter drop provided that you see to it that it doesn't happen again. We won't be lenient a second time.'

'I—you're letting him go . . .'

'As long as I have your assurance that you'll keep him under control. I'm calling all their parents and saying the same thing. In view of their age . . .'

'Their age . . . I don't understand. Who are you?'

'Didn't our detective explain?'

'No.'

'I see. I'm the manager of—' He named the department store. The one where they'd bought all the children's school things. He hadn't been kidnapped. It was all right! He almost laughed, but the voice on the other end was still talking.

'We've had our eye on this little band for some weeks. Every Monday at the same time. They've got away with a bit of stuff, so we had to put a stop to it. Your boy had a sweater hidden, stuffed up under his jacket when the detective brought him to me.'

The new blow made the Marshal's heart thump so loud he could hear it, but this time he was able to think. He was coping.

'He hadn't tried to leave the store?'

'No. We stopped him right there near the counter.'

'Then legally speaking he hasn't stolen anything.'

The voice at the other end grew angry. 'I'm doing you a favour, I thought you'd have understood that. My detective could have let him get as far as the door and arrested him the minute he stepped outside!'

'Yes, I do realize. I understand. Thank you.'

'I'll send him off home, then.' The voice was still offended.

'I—no! Don't . . . I'd rather one of us came for him.' What if Totò was so scared he tried to run away?

'We're already closed for lunch. If it hadn't been for this I'd have been gone half an hour ago.'

The man must be placated. He mustn't let Totò leave alone.

'We'll come in the car. I promise you we'll be there in five minutes. You understand, I'm afraid he may be so frightened that he won't come home.'

'Hm. Well, you may be right. He's in a bad state. Five minutes, then . . .'

The five minutes seemed to last an hour. Giovanni, who was already home, came out of his bedroom to ask, 'What's happening?' Teresa, terrified, her coat flung over her apron, refused to get in the car until he had sworn that Totò hadn't had a road accident. But how could he tell her in the house with Giovanni listening in? So he told her in the car during that interminable five minutes. When they arrived she was white with shock and they collected the tearful Totò without her having said a word. The drive home went all too quickly. What should he say? What could he say? He was stunned and shaken, more from what he had first thought was happening than from what had really happened.

He was only too relieved when, on their entering the flat, Totò sprang loose from his mother's grasp and shot into the bedroom, slamming the door behind him. Even so, it couldn't be put off for ever, and this time there was no leaving it to Teresa who was staring at him, dumb with fear.

He took his coat off and hung it up slowly.

'It's all right. I'll talk to him.'

'You won't . . .'

'Won't what?' Surely she didn't think he'd hit the child?

He'd never laid a finger on either of the boys. It had always been Teresa who'd given them a slap when necessary. Nevertheless, she was looking at him fearfully.

'You won't get too angry? What an awful thing to happen . . .'

He knew exactly what she meant. To someone in his position it *was* an awful thing to happen. She looked anxiously into his face. 'It's just that you look . . . Don't frighten him too much, Salva. It's serious, but the main thing is to get to the bottom of it, to try and understand.'

'Don't worry.'

'Just don't come down too heavily, or else—'

'All right!'

This was no time to explain to her that it was the fright he'd had that had reduced him to this state. He opened the door of the boys' room. Totò was seated stiffly on the very edge of his bed, his face blanched and dirty with tears. He looked as if he were having difficulty breathing. Giovanni was standing looking at him. He must have been asking him what was wrong, but he turned when his father entered and fell silent. Without being asked to, he left the room, not having found out anything but sensing something dreadful that made him glad to leave. Once they were alone, it became even clearer that Totò was having trouble breathing. His thin chest was heaving and each forced shallow breath was audible in the ensuing silence.

'Well . . .' Where to start? Ask him why he'd tried to steal a small child's sweater that could be of no use to him or anyone? What was the point? Then something occurred to him that he could and should ask. 'How come you were there, in the centre of town? Why weren't you at school?'

'It's Monday.' His voice was shallow and tremulous.

'So?'

'We're supposed to go to gymnastics last thing before lunch . . . it's across town.'

'You mean you were on your way there?'

Totò's fear had gone beyond any hope of extricating himself with lies. 'We never go. We hang around in the centre.'

'Why? *Why?*'

'It's stupid! It's miles to get there and then there's only about twenty minutes of lesson left, running round in that stupid little gym with no equipment! And anyway, we're always hungry. We get slices of pizza—well, it's nearly half past two when we get back for lunch! It's stupid!'

Where had he heard all this before? It brought to mind the face of a bossy woman with glasses . . . Parents' night. Hadn't she talked of some sort of petition? And yet he hadn't seen it that he could remember . . .

'*It's no wonder some of them are skipping off.*' The words came back to him with sudden clarity. '*It's no wonder—*'

'You've been skipping gymnastics every week, is that it?'

'Everybody does.'

'"Everybody" being this group you go about with?'

Totò didn't answer.

'And does "*everybody*" steal from the department store?'

The child's voice dropped to a hoarse whisper. 'We took turns.'

'And today was your turn?'

He nodded.

'What did the others pinch?'

'Nothing much. Pencils, toffees off the stand near the cash desk.'

'Toffees! But you had to do better than that and steal a sweater. For God's sake—'

'It's your fault! It's all your fault! I wouldn't have done it if it hadn't been for you! I'm fed up with being laughed at and tormented because my dad's a carabiniere! I'm fed up!' He was screaming hysterically, his eyes dry and bright. 'And they laugh at Giovanni as well, they laugh at Giovanni! Everybody says we're soft, that we're such goodie-goodies that we daren't even walk up a one-way street the wrong way. It's *you*! They take the mickey out of us because of you! Why can't you get a real job like everybody else's dad? Other people's dads earn stacks of money and have real houses. Real houses, not like this dump. I don't want to live in a barracks where my friends won't come because of you and your stupid horrible uniform. I hate you! I hate you! I hate you!'

And he flung his small body at the Marshal's great bulk, thumping with his fist at the offending gold buttons.

'Totò!' Teresa, unable to stand it any longer, burst into the room. Totò flung himself on the bed choking with dry sobs and she ran to sit beside him. 'Totò! What's happened?'

The Marshal walked out without a word. He went straight to the kitchen and poured himself a glass of water from the jug on the table that was set for lunch. He didn't sit down but drank it standing at the window, staring out, seeing nothing. There was a bad smell and after a moment he opened the window. Rain came in, spattering the sink and sometimes wetting his face. He didn't move. Only after a long time when the smell got worse despite the open window, did he realize that something was burning on the stove. He turned it off. It looked like olive oil but it was black and smoking. He went into the hall, got his hat and coat and walked out.

He walked for a long time, making automatically for the river, perhaps feeling in need of a more open space, more air to breathe, but without any real direction. He was vaguely conscious of some severe pain in his stomach. Not hunger; he felt as though he'd been kicked. He was walking much faster than usual through the rainy streets emptied for the lunch-hour. Walking like someone driven, conscious only of his feet thudding and splashing on the wet paving stones. His mind remained a blank until he reached a bridge and then he stood in the centre of it, looking over the low parapet at the swollen river, brown and oily, flowing fast towards Pisa.

The water churned and splashed below him as the rain fell steadily into it. He wanted to keep his mind empty, to block out Totò's streaked white face, the eyes bright with hatred. He succeeded in keeping it at a distance but other distressing images came in its place: Lulu's half-shaved head turning to reveal a creased and flattened smile; a puny child of ten with great circles under his eyes trying to sell cigarettes in the hot darkness of summer nights down home . . . at that age . . . At that age, when there was no school he sometimes got to go with his father to the market in the village. And when his business was done they'd go into the bar in the piazza where all the other men were sitting . . . what made him think of it now? That was it. The village marshal would almost always walk in at some point and the men would raise their caps, some of them half stand.

'Good morning, Marshal.'

The marshal. A respected man. The priest, the marshal, the local magistrate, respected men. And now? He must have been aware, at least at the back of his mind, how much things had changed, but the image of the village marshal, whose name he couldn't even remember, had remained fixed until the instant when Totò had demolished it with a few childish words. Totò . . . he didn't want to think about it yet. Down river to the right the first trees of the Cascine were invisible, shrouded in rain. Somewhere beyond them Peppina's sopping fur might still . . . Image followed image, each more miserable than the last in a miserable rain-sodden world, as if the whole city were weeping. The little black cat flung dead at his feet . . . Carla, sleeping by now, her misery kept away by drugs, waiting to attack as soon as she opened her eyes. Was there nobody who was happy? He thought at once of Ferrini. He'd never seen Ferrini depressed. He was cheerful even in the most unpromising circumstances. At the thought he turned away from the

brown water and crossed the bridge. In a few minutes he
was in Borgo Ognissanti. Dark blue cars were nosing out of
the entrance, windscreen-wipers already on, turning right.
The two men on duty were sheltering just inside the great
doors. He stepped in and bent to speak through the glass
window on the right where a youngster manned the switch-
board.

'Ferrini? Sorry, no. I saw him leave myself with his wife
—probably gone out to lunch. He'll be in his office at
five.'

Of course. It was lunch-time. He hadn't thought . . .

'Do you want to leave a message for him?'

'No, no . . .'

He didn't go away but went along the old cloister. The
thought of the cheery Ferrini out at lunch with his wife
didn't make him feel better at all, only accentuated his
depression. The best thing might be to do something useful,
or at least to turn his mind to someone worse off than
himself.

It wasn't so easy, at that time of day, to find someone to
let him in, but he insisted. Peppina was lying face down on
the bunk but his eyes were open. His tangled blond hair,
darkening now at the roots, was stuck to his forehead with
sweat. The hot little cell stank of sweat and fear and stale
cigarette smoke. Peppina turned his head a little as the
Marshal came in but didn't raise it. His voice was hoarse
and languid.

'Are they going to move me?'

'I don't know.'

'Why are you here, then?'

He didn't know that either but he pulled forward the only
chair and sat down with his hat on his knees. His soaked
greatcoat began to steam.

'Tell me what happened that night.'

'I've told you. I've told them all. I'm tired . . .'

'Tell me again.'

'There's nothing else to tell. What do you want from me?'
He turned his face to the wall.

'I want help from you.'

The only response was a grunt of disgust.

'I want to find Nanny.'

That made him turn back. He propped himself up on one elbow.

'Nobody believes Nanny even exists! Why should you—'

'Because I know he does exist. I've seen a photograph of him.'

'I don't know his real name, if that's what you want.'

'I know you don't. I'll still find him. Florence isn't such a big city and I have that photograph.'

'He doesn't live in Florence.'

'You know that? Why didn't you say so?'

'Because nobody asked me! They didn't believe a fucking word I said, did they? Well, did they?'

'Try and keep calm.'

'I feel ill. I haven't slept. Last night I took two sleeping pills and all they did was give me nightmares. I couldn't fall asleep and I couldn't keep properly awake. Just nightmares for hours. You can't imagine—'

'Start at the beginning and tell me again.'

'If you say so. I ate at the trattoria—whether they say so or not, I did—'

'Never mind that. Go on.'

'I went to work about half past eleven. I was in my usual place where you picked me up—'

'How did you get there?'

'To the Cascine? By taxi, same as always.'

'Then the taxi-driver will confirm it.'

'He will if he feels like it, for what difference it makes.'

'Go on.'

'Nanny turned up. I don't know what time but I hadn't been there long.'

'Turned up on foot or in a car?'

'In his car—then you really do believe me?'

'What happened then? What did he say?'

'That . . . that Lulu had left for Spain. He was pissed off. He asked me to go back to the flat with him.'

'What for?'

'What do you think?'

'And did . . .?'

'No. I told you he was pissed off. When we got there he said he just wanted to talk but that he'd pay me. He put a record on and we had a drink.'

'What did you talk about?'

'About Lulu mostly. She was the biggest bitch of all time but he was always crazy about her.'

'Was he over-excited? Did he seem to behave oddly?'

'No. He was very quiet.'

'He told you Lulu had gone to Spain—but he didn't look upset?'

'Why should he be? She'd only gone to the clinic, she was coming back. I thought he looked a bit tired but he was calm enough.'

'Where did all this take place? The drinks and music, in the sitting-room?'

'That's right.'

'The whole time?'

'I told you, we didn't—'

'I just want to know if you went in any of the other rooms. The kitchen, for instance. Did you see that anyone had eaten there?'

'I didn't go in the kitchen—Wait! He did. Nanny—he went to get a bottle of water from the fridge. We drank whisky.'

'You didn't glance in there? You didn't notice the table?'

'No. I was pouring the whisky.'

'What about the other rooms?'

'I didn't go wandering about the place. We were only there about a quarter of an hour, long enough to have a drink. Then I reminded him he'd promised to pay me.'

'And he gave you those traveller's cheques? Listen, I can only help you if you tell me the truth.'

'I am telling the truth! You're just as bad as the rest of the bastards! Why will nobody believe me?'

'Keep your voice down. I'm not saying I don't believe he gave you the cheques, I'm only saying that if he did you must have known something was up unless he gave you a good explanation. Why should Lulu have left them behind —and what about the amount? You're not trying to tell me that you'd ever been paid that much for a quarter of an hour? Well?'

'I knew it was too much. I knew that. I thought he did it just to spite her, seeing as it was her money and not his —and why should I have cared? He said she had more money than she knew what to do with, that she'd left it behind. It was obvious enough that it was stolen from her, but I needed it. It wasn't my problem if he had troubles with Lulu, and I needed it!'

'To set up your business?'

'Yes. Nanny knew that. He said he wanted to help me. The shit!'

'What do you know about him?'

'I don't know ... nothing much except that he was always after Lulu like the rest of them ... and his kid. I never heard him mention his wife but he was crazy about this kid of his.'

'Nothing else?'

'No. Yes ... he'd been staying in Lulu's flat for a bit. He must have been because there were a lot of his clothes and stuff in the bedroom.'

'You said you didn't go in the other rooms.'

'I forgot. I went in the bedroom before we left, to powder my nose.'

He watched Peppina's face carefully as he asked, 'Did you use the bathroom?'

Not a flicker. There had been nothing in the papers yet about the blood found there. Peppina was picking at his chipped red nail varnish. 'No . . . He was in there, I remember. He went for a pee. He was in there talking to himself, muttering about Lulu.'

'Saying what?'

'I don't know, I wasn't listening. Something about "coming back" and I heard him say Lulu's name, that's all —Christ! You don't think that bitch was in there hiding, listening to it all?'

'I think she was dead by then.' But where the devil was the body? In the wardrobe? It was all too bizarre.

'Anyway, then we left. There's really nothing against me, is there,' Peppina said, 'except that money, that and what I am. Christ, why did I ever take it? Why did I?'

'For your own good, try and keep calm. Anything you tell me could be important. If you don't keep calm you won't remember.'

There was little point in telling him that there was more against him than just the money. There were the fingerprints in the flat, not yet confirmed but they would be. That and the hopeless task—whatever he'd said to the contrary— of finding the wretched Nanny who could so easily deny everything.

'What's the use?' Peppina said, dropping his head again, as if reading his thoughts. 'There's nothing else to remember. He drove me back to my place in the Cascine and left me.'

'Do you know where he went?'

'Home. He said he was going home, that he wanted to see his kid. That was the last I saw of him. You're wasting your time, you know that? I'll never get out . . . I don't care any more. I wouldn't care if only I could sleep . . . Will you do me a favour?'

'If I can.'

'In my bag, there on the floor somewhere. There are two prescriptions in it. I don't know who else to ask.'

He found the prescriptions and slipped them in his pocket.

'I just want to sleep . . .'

Outside it was still raining. After the heat of the basement the Marshal shivered in his damp clothes. He turned up his collar but it felt wet and sharp against his face. After crossing the river he had to hang about for a bit in the bar in Piazza San Felice until the chemist next door opened up. As it happened, the chemist himself, handsome, spruce and cheerful, appeared in the bar wanting a coffee before starting work.

''Afternoon, Marshal! You look as though you might be waiting for me. What have you been doing to your face?'

'I—nothing. It's nothing. I was waiting for you, though.'

'If it's urgent—'

'No. Have your coffee.'

'Right you are. Can I offer you something?'

'I've ordered.'

They drank up and walked next door together. The Marshal produced the two prescriptions and the chemist disappeared into the back room. When he came back he was staring with a puzzled look at the boxes in his hand.

'What do you want with this stuff?'

'I don't even know what it is.'

'This one's sleeping pills, but this other's a hormone usually given to women threatening to miscarry—'

'They're not for me. I'm just doing somebody a favour.'

'I see. I was worried about your wife for a minute. Eight thousand seven-fifty to you. And let's hope this rain doesn't keep up.'

The Marshal left and began walking slowly through Piazza Pitti in spite of the steady downpour. He would arrive only in time to go straight into his office at five. It must be nearly that now. The traffic was already thick,

swishing slowly through the rain. Most of the cars had their
lights on.

'Marshal!'

He stopped and looked about him.

'Marshal! Over here!' He spotted an old lady of the
Quarter whom he knew quite well. She was waving at him
frantically from the other side of the square. He pushed his
way between the barely moving cars and went over to her.
She was very tiny and her raincoat came almost down to
her feet.

'You'll have to help me,' she said, 'I can't manage on my
own. Look.' They were in front of a travel agent's shop. It
had two windows and between them in the space before the
door the usual metal shutter was pulled down. The lower
part of the shutter was of solid horizontal strips but the rest
was a sort of lattice-work. Behind the shutter sat an orange
and white cat looking up at them hopefully. On the floor
beside it was a bit of butcher's paper with some mincemeat
on it.

'Poor little thing! Poor little kitty!' crooned Pierina. Her
hand which she poked through the lattice grille was wet and
scratched. The cat ran forward and sniffed at it eagerly,
purring.

'You see? She wants me to help her but I can't manage.'

'Well, it's dry enough in there and surely they'll open up
at five.'

'No, no! It's not their cat and don't you see the notice?'

In fact, there was a paper stuck on the glass door beyond
the grille among the credit card signs which said 'Closed
for renovation'.

'She must have managed to climb in somehow to shelter
from the rain and now she can't get out.'

'But there's food there,' the Marshal said.

'I poked it through,' Pierina said. 'But I can't get a saucer
of water through. I've tried. We have to get her out.' The
rain was running down her distressed face. Goodness knew

how long she'd been struggling there and she was a frail creature to be hanging about in such weather. The Marshal knew she suffered badly from bronchitis and her neighbours were sure each year that one more winter would carry her off, but she was tough in her own way and struggled on. The saucer she had brought was parked on the doorstep in front of the metal shutter with the rain splashing into it.

'Well,' he said, 'if she got in she should be able to get out.' He bent down and was just able to get his big hand through the grille. Again the cat ran forward, purring. He got hold of it near the scruff of its neck and pulled it up to the first row of latticed holes. Its head came through but then, because its shoulders were wider and because it was impossible for both the Marshal's hand and the cat to come through the same hole, they were stuck. The dangling cat began to panic and scratch and he had to let it drop. It sat down again immediately as though nothing had happened and stared up at them. It didn't touch Pierina's bit of mincemeat.

'You see,' she said. 'That's what happens when I try. Poor little creature—you're not going?' She had seen the Marshal glance at his watch.

'No, no, don't worry.' He tried again, but as soon as the cat got stuck she panicked and tore back so that he had to drop her. His hand was a mass of wet scratches but he didn't give up. Surely he could get one thing right today, relieve one bit of misery, however small.

'I can't help her if she won't cooperate . . . she starts pulling back as soon as she feels the grille.'

'She's frightened, poor thing.'

They crouched there, side by side, the rain pattering steadily on their backs, the cars splashing filthy water at them, as they repeated the process time after time without results. And yet each time the orange and white cat ran forward purring to the hand that reached out to it uselessly.

'My hand's smaller,' Pierina said. 'Shall I have another try?'

'Wait. We must think of some other way ... You get hold of her this time, under the armpits, if you know what I mean, and I'll put my hand through the next hole and try and push her from behind ... Have you got her? Right, pull!'

And it worked. All three of them were pleased. Pierina held the loudly purring creature close to her wet coat.

'There! Now you're safe. I only wish I could take you home but my Robbi would see you off.' She looked up at the Marshal and said, 'I'd better take her back to Boboli.'

'Is that where she's from?' The Boboli Gardens behind the Pitti Palace were full of cats of all shapes and sizes who survived mostly on the leavings of tourists and the goodwill of old women like Pierina.

'That's where she's from, all right. Poor creature, my coat's making you wet, isn't it?'

'I'll take her back, if she's from Boboli,' the Marshal said. 'I'm going back to my office now—and you should go home and get dry or you'll catch a chill.' He took the purring cat from her and buttoned it into the front of his greatcoat from where it peered out contentedly at the rainy world. Pierina picked up her saucer and emptied it. Then her tiny thin fingers clutched the Marshal's big hand. 'Thank you.'

He crossed the road and went up the sloping forecourt in front of the Palace. By the time he turned left at the top to go under the stone arch, he could feel the animal's warmth penetrating his thick uniform. Nevertheless, by the time he got up the stairs and unlocked the door he had quite forgotten it. He had quite forgotten, too, his resolution not to go to his quarters but straight to his office. He was thinking of Carla and the unlucky little Mishi, thinking too that he should also change his clothes as he was even wetter than old Pierina had been. So he was vaguely surprised when Teresa, after the obvious comment, 'Salva! You're soaked!' peered at him more closely and said, 'Whatever have you got there?'

'A cat,' he said, remembering. He looked down. Only the very top of its head and its white ears were visible. It seemed to be asleep. He unbuttoned his wet coat. 'I meant to leave it downstairs with the park keeper.'

'You'd better change first.' The boys were out of sight and she made no mention of what had happened, but the atmosphere was strained. They talked over it. She took the cat from him and he went to the bedroom to change. Even his socks were wet. When he was dressed again and tying his tie, Teresa came into the bedroom and whispered, 'Salva . . .'

'What?' He wished she wouldn't. He couldn't face it yet.

'I've had a talk with him. He's very upset, you know.'

'I know.' She might have thought that he too was upset, but he didn't say so.

'Well, it's all come out. You know how attached he was to Leonardo last year. He was his first friend—they were both a bit lost, he and Giovanni, when they first came up from down home. Anyway, it seems—' she was still whispering, so the boys must have been next door in their room—'Leonardo's parents are . . . well, you know the type, active in '68, that sort of thing and very anti-army. Anyway, they must have said something, I don't know what, and Leonardo found another friend and dropped Totò completely. That's what started the trouble. You know, once these things come to a head they fade away. I'm sure he'll settle down now. I've had a long talk to him and he knows the first thing he must do is apologize to you.'

'No. I don't want . . . Leave him be.'

'But, Salva, it's only right—'

'Not just now. If you say it's sorted out, that's enough. I don't want him being forced to apologize.'

She stared at him, not understanding his hurt or his embarrassment. Before she could say anything they were interrupted by Giovanni shouting, 'Mum! Mum! There's a cat in the kitchen!'

They went in there and found Giovanni holding the orange and white cat in his arms, his eyes alight. 'Where's it come from? Is it for us?'

'No, no,' the Marshal said, 'it's just a stray from Boboli. I have to give it to the park keeper downstairs.' He was glad he'd forgotten. It provided a distraction.

'Can I give it some milk, Mum?'

'If you like . . .' With a swift glance at her husband she added, 'Go and tell Totò. You can both give it some milk.'

When Totò appeared, the Marshal all but kept his back turned to him, not wanting to catch his eye.

The boy bent down to stroke the cat, which purred loudly and rubbed itself against him. He too said, 'Is it for us?'

'No. It's a stray from Boboli.'

Giovanni poured some milk into a saucer and put it on the floor. The cat sniffed at it cautiously and then settled nearer and began to lap it up. Teresa switched the light on. It was warm in the kitchen and there was a newly baked cake on the table. The shutters were closed against the rain. When the cat had licked the saucer clean, Giovanni picked it up again.

'Let me hold it,' Totò said. 'You held it before.' He took it in his thin arms and stroked it. 'It's purring, I can feel it.'

'Hear it, you mean,' said Giovanni.

'I can feel it as well. It's thin, isn't it, Mum?'

'That's because it's a stray.'

'Why can't we keep it?'

'Because it's a stray,' the Marshal said, 'and it could have all sorts of diseases.'

'We could take it to the vet.' Totò was still looking at his mother, avoiding his father's eyes.'

'Well . . . it looks healthy enough . . .' Teresa hazarded.

'Cats are for the country,' the Marshal said, 'where they

can run about. It's not right to keep animals cooped up in flats in the city.'

'It could still play in Boboli!' Totò's eyes were filling up.

'It'll run off. It's wild.'

'I could find it again. I know where they play, near the fish pond where the tourists sit to eat their sandwiches, I've seen them. I want to keep it and get a basket for it! It's thin and lonely.' Totò began to cry in earnest, his face already white from his upset, sobbing for his own misery in the name of the cat that he clutched with all his might. All at once he put it down on the floor and ran, still sobbing, to the bedroom.

'It's not right,' the Marshal repeated.

But Giovanni and Teresa were both looking at him as though he were the hangman.

'I'm going to do my homework,' Giovanni said. He walked out without a word to his father.

'There's no need for you all to turn on me,' the Marshal protested. 'It's not right to keep animals in a flat.'

'One animal. One small cat. We weren't thinking of opening a zoo.'

He picked up the cat, which started to purr again at once.

'Shouldn't you be back in the office? I've got to wash this floor if you've finished in here.'

'I thought at least you would know I was talking sense. You at least should realize that it's not right—'

'All right. Do what you think fit. Take the wretched cat away.'

But as he left he heard her mutter, 'What's right isn't always what's good.'

So what was that supposed to mean?

CHAPTER 8

'His age?'

'I don't know his age, only the name and that he lives in Milan. He may be some sort of commercial traveller—at any rate he does a job that brings him fairly often to Florence, or used to.'

'Well, if all you want is his place of residence I can get that from the town hall—if he's still here . . . Nearly a year ago, you said?'

'It may not be very accurate . . .' The Marshal wasn't all that sure if the address was all he wanted. He'd picked up the phone the minute he'd walked into his office, wanting to plunge himself into work so as not to give himself any time to think.

'Wait,' he added. 'One other thing—his civil status. I'd be very interested to know if he's become divorced or separated during the last year.'

'Divorced or separated . . . I've made a note. What about any previous convictions? Interested?'

'No. Yes . . . I suppose you'd better check but it's unlikely. I think you'll find he's a respectable man.'

Only after putting the phone down did he hear an echo of the irony that had been in his voice when he said it. 'A respectable man.' It no longer meant anything to him. He'd come across a lot of 'respectable' people during this case. A respectable bourgeoise landlady who 'didn't know' Lulu was a transsexual, this undoubtedly respectable Milanese businessman whom Lulu had blackmailed, the respectable jeweller who had given Titi a diamond ring and claimed it back on his theft insurance, and all the others . . . night after night queuing in their cars by the hundred in the lamplit park. All of them respectable men and most of them with wives and children. It didn't mean what it had once meant to him . . . the priest, the marshal, the local magistrate. 'Other people's dads make stacks of money . . .' Was that all it came down to? Totò—but he didn't want to think about that. He picked up the phone again.

'Ferrini.'

Thank goodness for that. 'Guarnaccia speaking. Come over to Pitti, will you? I need to talk to you.'

'To Pitti?' There was an uncomfortable silence before he went on. 'I . . . well, I'd better ask the Captain . . .'

'Ask . . . What do you mean? You're still on this case with me, aren't you—they haven't replaced you?'

'No.'

'Well, then?'

'They haven't replaced me but I've been taken off it, even so. Surely you expected—Once Peppina was inside. I imagine the Prosecutor thought you didn't need extra help any more, so . . . If you like I'll talk to the Captain, but I don't think—'

'I'll talk to him myself.'

He had dialled again and the number was ringing when he put a finger on the receiver rest to stop it. He ought to think first, have his story ready. Ferrini was right, as usual. He should have expected it. As far as the Prosecutor was concerned, the case was virtually solved. Peppina was inside. A charge had been brought and the search was off. What need had he officially for Ferrini?

He sat there for over five minutes, staring at the map of his Quarter on the wall facing his desk, trying to think of a story, his finger still parked on the receiver rest. Then he let go and dialled. He hadn't thought of anything and he never would, not if he sat there until tomorrow. Thinking wasn't his strong point, he wasn't equipped for it. You needed brains, and the one who had the brains was the Captain. The number rang.

'Maestrangelo.'

'Captain, Guarnaccia speaking.'

'Ah, Marshal. Everything going all right?'

'No.'

'Oh . . .'

'Hmph! No, sir. I need Ferrini.' Well, there was no point in beating about the bush. He had to have what he needed and the Captain must get it for him. That was all there was to it.

'Ferrini . . . one of the two men I put on the case with you . . .'

'I just want Ferrini.'

'The Public Prosecutor gave me to understand that the case was—'

'Yes, sir. He's brought a charge.'

'And you're still as unconvinced. Guarnaccia, remember what I said to you earlier.'

'Yes, sir. That's what settled it. I mean, I had my doubts before but it was what you said about it being a cold-blooded killing. It must have been carefully planned and carried out over a period of some hours at least, maybe two days. Peppina's unbalanced, hot-tempered, impulsive.'

'I said all that? You don't have some other suspect up your sleeve, by any chance?'

'Yes, but I don't know where he is.'

'Not the mythical witness, I hope?'

'No. But I want to find him, too. The man I'm after had a serious grudge against Lulu. Blackmail. It may well have ruined his life.'

'In that case— Have you informed the Prosecutor?'

'I'd rather find the man first, otherwise . . .' There was no need to go on. He knew the Captain's feeling about the anomalous function of the Prosecutor who was meant to act as an impartial judge during the inquiry and then to appear in court for the prosecution. He wasn't going to kill himself looking for a witness who would demolish his court case. They would have to present him with an alternative to

Peppina before he'd move. He waited, letting the Captain chew this over before adding, 'You chose a good man in Ferrini. Give him back to me and I'll find this man.'

'All right, Guarnaccia. I'll call the Prosecutor now and see what I can do.'

'You won't—'

'Leave it to me. I'll tell him you're overworked over there already and that you've never run a case on your own—well, anyway, I'll think of something.'

'Thanks.'

'I'll call you back.'

And the Marshal stared at the map on the wall for another seven minutes. When the Captain called back with the good news he ended with a word of warning.

'Just one thing, Guarnaccia: it's just as well that you're the blue-eyed boy with the Prosecutor for the moment, but from now on you're on your own. Whatever you're up to I don't know about it.'

'Yes, sir. I understand.'

'And good luck.'

'Thanks.'

He no longer stared at the map while he waited. Instead, he went through the autopsy report again. He was half way through when Ferrini knocked and walked in.

'Got it, sir!' Bruno's eyes were alight when he burst in on them.

'Don't call me sir.'

'Sorry, Marshal. But what a piece of luck!'

'We could do with some of that,' remarked Ferrini.

'You found him?'

'Better than that! Here's his taxi number and the name —he picked up Peppina at the trattoria at eleven-forty that night. Here's the record of the call. He took him to his usual place down the park, as you said.'

'How can he be so sure it was Peppina? This just records the time and the run.'

'That's not all, sir—Marshal! He gave me this.' Bruno offered the Marshal a small slip of paper. 'Peppina was broke after the restaurant bill and couldn't pay. The driver filled this out—Peppina should have a copy—anyway, he never got paid but wasn't too worried. He said it happened all the time but they always pay up when they're in funds. He was just biding his time until he picked him up again.'

'Only we picked him up instead,' Ferrini said. 'What a half-wit not to realize he had the makings of an alibi.'

'Anything else you want me to do, Marshal?'

'No—Yes. Take this package of medicine over to Borgo Ognissanti and see it's given to the man in the cells. Take some cigarettes, too.'

When he'd gone they looked at each other.

'It looks as though you might be right,' Ferrini said.

'It doesn't much matter,' the Marshal pointed out, 'whether I am or not. Peppina's not off the hook yet but if he did it, well, he's inside and nothing lost. So let's say he didn't. Let's say he's telling the truth—and can you imagine anybody preparing a story like his beforehand and leaving out this slip of paper?'

'Or even cleaning that bathroom so nicely?' Ferrini grinned. 'All right. I'm with you. But the timing of it . . .'

'Yes, that's the trouble.'

'Let's go back over it—assuming Peppina's story's true. Somewhere around midnight he was in the flat with Nanny and there doesn't seem to have been a dead body floating about, so it either happened long before and Professor Forli's losing his grip, or afterwards.'

'Afterwards . . .' The Marshal thought a bit and then said, 'If it was afterwards—even the meal.'

'Could have been. They eat at all hours, not your nine-to-fivers.'

'That's true.'

'Menu,' announced Ferrini, taking up the report on the contents of Lulu's stomach: 'fried chicken breast, salad, bread, shop-bought chocolate ice-cream cake, red wine, sleeping pill. Lovely!'

'But before . . . If Lulu didn't leave for Spain but Nanny thought differently . . .'

'You can't be sure of that—are we believing *everything* Peppina says?'

'I don't know. Yes. For the moment, yes.'

'Well, one of the things he says is that Nanny's stuff was all over the bedroom, right?'

'Yes.'

'So if it's true he said he was going home when he left Peppina in the park—well, we didn't find any men's stuff.'

'He'd have gone back . . .'

'And I wonder what he found? Lulu? Lulu plus pal from Milan? A dinner party? A corpse?'

'He could have disturbed the murderer, it's true.'

'Who ran off and came back with his saw in the morning! I hope you're not thinking of telling the Prosecutor all this. We'd both get transferred to Palermo.'

'No,' the Marshal said, 'I'm not telling him anything, not yet . . . They should call me from Milan . . .'

They called. Ferrini watched the Marshal's face as he answered, but as always it was expressionless and told him nothing. So he listened, his face puzzled.

'Speaking . . . Yes. Good—the address? I see . . . I see. No, I hadn't thought of it but . . . Wait—when exactly? I see. No, there's no point. Leave it at that. Thanks.'

The Marshal replaced the receiver and rubbed a hand over his still expressionless face.

'Moved, has he?' Ferrini's voice had a touch of impatience at the Marshal's slowness. 'Left the country?'

'No, no . . .' He slumped back in his chair. 'A road accident almost a year ago. Who knows? Maybe he was driving home from here after the upset with Lulu. It happened on the motorway. Anyway, he's dead.'

'Dead . . . Well, that's that, then.'

'Yes.'

'What are you going to do now?'

'Find Nanny.' The Marshal stood up. 'We'll set off now. And I hope you've got a raincoat.'

They took with them Ferrini's list of all the transsexuals in the city. All two hundred and odd of them.

They woke them from their drugged daytime sleep, bleary-eyed and sullen, unable to talk or even to listen until they'd had a coffee, a cigarette, a glass of sugared water. They felt too tired, too sickly or too muddle-headed to remember. The questions were always the same.

Do you know the man they call Nanny?'

Do you know his real name?

Even just his first name?

How tall is he? Taller than me? Than Ferrini?

They interrupted them at their toilette, dressing-gowns pulled around exotic underwear, white lace, black chiffon, red satin. They did their best but were in a hurry and had to carry on, listening as they peered and preened, brushed and painted and sprayed, answering in monosyllables or with only a shrug.

Did he have any distinguishing marks?

A prominent mole, a birthmark, a tattoo?

Did he have a Florentine accent?

Any accent at all?

Any speech impediment?

Later, when they began to find nobody at home, they went to the four or five trattorie where they met to eat in little groups, interrupting them as they wound their spaghetti, poured more wine, stubbed out cigarettes, sometimes in full ashtrays, sometimes in the remains of food they couldn't get down. They gave what answers they could, disputing among themselves or with enemy groups at other tables, their gaudy clothes and masculine voices attracting amused attention from dining couples and families.

Did he go with anyone else besides Carla and then Lulu? Have you seen him around recently?

When?

Before Lulu's death or after?

In the daytime or only at night?

Later still, after seeing so much food, Ferrini suggested eating and supposed that the Marshal would prefer to go home and meet later. The Marshal, to his surprise, didn't want to go home. They ate together in a smallish place that was about to close, where one waiter served them grudgingly and another started stacking chairs and sweeping before they'd finished. Their clothes were soaked, as Ferrini pointed out, and he asked where they were going next, hoping he'd say 'home'.

'To the Cascine.' And they set out again in the rain.

They approached them under dripping trees in the shadows and under umbrellas beneath the white-globed lamps. They stopped them getting into cars and were waiting for them when they got out.

Did you get the impression he was rich?

From his clothes, his car?

What make of car was it? What colour?

Was it a Florentine number plate?

Only when the rain was falling on the deserted wet black avenues of the park did they give up and go home. All they had found out, after questioning almost seventy people, was that Nanny's car, which was large and expensive and either beige or red or dark blue or black, might have had a Florentine number. Ferrini had caught a cold.

After three days of unrelenting rain, when the Arno was boiling angrily through the city and people were pausing to glance at the danger level marked under the Santa Trinita bridge, Ferrini's cold developed into Chinese 'flu and the Marshal had eaten no meal except breakfast at home.

'There are only nineteen of them left,' Ferrini said, swilling down two more aspirins and consulting the list on the Marshal's desk. He'd made a tentative suggestion the day before that it might be worth trying to get the Prosecutor's approval of what they were doing so that they could officially haul the remaining transsexuals into the barracks and save themselves time and energy.

The Marshal had said no. He didn't give any explanation, knowing that Ferrini would assume he wanted to avoid annoying the Prosecutor. Perhaps that was even partly the case. But at the back of his mind were the words one of them, he couldn't remember who, had shouted at Ferrini that first night. *'If a nun gets murdered do you break into the convent at three in the morning and drag the other nuns round here for a going-over?'*

He'd been too embarrassed and distracted to take it in at the time, but he'd taken it in by now all right. So all he said was no.

Ferrini was looking at him now, waiting for some sort of decision. Up till now he had just moved doggedly ahead because he didn't know what else to do, without thinking, without hoping, without reacting. Now, quite suddenly, tired and disgusted, mostly with himself, he lost impetus. It was against every rule of a policeman's work. If you have to question a hundred people you question a hundred people. You don't give up after the ninety-ninth. The probability of the first person's giving you what you're after is no greater or less than that of its being the last. There was no case for being more hopeful at number ten than at number ninety. It meant nothing. He was just tired, that was all. And Ferrini was ill. He glanced at the window. It was still raining.

'They say we're due for a change,' Ferrini offered, catching his glance, 'and I suppose it can hardly be a change for the worse.'

'No . . .'

'You look the way I feel. You shouldn't drink coffee after taking a lot of aspirin, should you?'

'No.'

'Pity. I could do with one. If I fall asleep in the car, give me a prod. Do you know something? I'm beginning to hate the guts of our friend Nanny. Do you realize that if he hadn't tarted himself up as a woman in that photograph—' he poked at it angrily with his finger—'we could have cut the other two off it and slapped it on the front of the newspaper. WILL THIS MAN PLEASE COME FORWARD?'

'He wouldn't have come.'

'No, but I'd have felt better. Well, shall we go?' He stood up and buttoned his raincoat.

'You wouldn't feel better.' The Marshal was staring at the photo. The man's ill-made-up face, Carla's dazed, slightly drunken stare, Lulu's dazzling smile. 'There's the wife, a child . . .'

'I know. I was just letting off steam. I wouldn't do that to anybody, especially not the child. I've got three myself. Imagine, what a thing to find out about your father.' He had lit a cigarette but, perhaps because of his 'flu or the aspirins, he at once made a grimace of distaste and stubbed it out in the ashtray which the Marshal had found for him when they'd first started working together. Still, the Marshal didn't move.

'What about the labs . . . Could they doctor it? I mean, clean up the face a bit, substitute another man's shoulders with ordinary clothes?'

'Easily. And he still wouldn't come forward. Even if we're only talking about a witness—and we can't be a hundred per cent sure of that, though he doesn't sound much like a suspect compared to our late friend from Milan—no married man could afford to risk being a witness to a case like this. Ruin his life. And think of the risk. With Peppina inside, wherever he is he feels safe. If he sees his picture in the paper, however cleaned up and under whatever pretext, he's bound to scarper.'

'Yes. I wasn't thinking of the paper. Just notifying our stations throughout the province . . .'

'That's a thought—or bung him in the missing persons' bulletin and cover the whole country just in case. It *is* a thought. Slow, mind you. We've missed this month's.'

The Marshal shrugged. 'We'll do both, anyway. Send it to all stations in Tuscany and get it into the bulletin.'

'Will you see to it or shall I?'

The Marshal frowned. He didn't answer straight away. Then he said, 'You do it . . .'

When Ferrini left, the Marshal sat on, trying to remember something. The missing persons' bulletin, for some reason he couldn't fathom, had some painful association for him that he couldn't name. What was it? Why should he not want to think of it? Something to do with that wretched kid from Syracuse? Unhappy as the thought was, it wasn't that. The little girl who got lost . . . but she'd never been put into the bulletin, her mother had come that day. That day . . . the day they'd last gone to the department store where Totò—that was why. He tried to dismiss the problem of Totò from his mind and think of work, but he couldn't. Nobody had mentioned the episode since, but though he had never been home long enough to know exactly how the land lay, he knew well that things weren't mended with Teresa after the cat business. He'd been getting home at four in the morning and the first two nights she'd pretended to be asleep. She always did do that on the rare occasions when he had to be out late but, given the way things were, he'd been offended. He'd even made a bit more noise getting to bed than he needed to, in the hope that she'd turn over and speak to him. Then last night she really had been asleep and he was even more offended. They couldn't just go on like that. This case wouldn't last for ever. Sometime life had to go back to normal, but already too much time had elapsed. The problem had gone under the surface and he had so little talent for talking about things that he would never be able to manœuvre it back to a level where it could be sorted out openly. What, when it came down to it, *did* he have any talent for? Not for solving a case like this, evidently. The first time he'd been given a case to run and a fine mess he'd made of it. The thing was completely out of control. It wasn't as though he'd made any sort of considered decision. Peppina hadn't been arrested because he in his great wisdom thought he was guilty. One minute he'd been bumbling around in the rainy darkness and the next minute a charge for murder had been brought against someone he was convinced was innocent. And now that he ought to be trying to get the thing back on the rails, here he sat worrying about his own problems instead of thinking about . . . What was he meant to be thinking about? Where had he been up to when his thoughts had rambled off . . . The bulletin. But that had turned out a dead end. Forget the bulletin. But he didn't. Not trusting even his memory, though it didn't often fail him, he got out the daily sheet for the date that the lost child had been brought in. There was nothing. Nothing at all. So why had he connected the two things? Perhaps he was just tired and muddled through lack of sleep. He slid the sheet back in place and was already thinking about Teresa again when it came to him that he just might have told her that the boy from Syracuse ought to be reported missing down there and that in doing so he might have mentioned the bulletin. So, at least that little mystery was solved.

'*There's a carabinieri station not two minutes away from your house.*'

He hadn't said that to Teresa? How could he have? The face he'd said it to appeared in his memory as a blur. An unpleasant face that he couldn't put a name to.

'*A friend recommended you.*'

That was it. He'd settled the dispute over the boundaries

of two gardens and this woman . . . a dreadful woman. Her son was missing.

He pulled the daily sheet out again and looked at the date. It was before they found Lulu, and he'd been missing some time if he remembered rightly. But who was he? What the devil was the awful woman's name? Hadn't he started typing the particulars before sending her away to report it somewhere else? He began searching through his drawers but he knew as he was doing it that there was no point. He could see himself quite clearly ripping it off the typewriter and throwing it away as he said, 'There's a carabinieri station not two minutes away from your house.' But where? Something like Via dei Fossi . . . or was Fossi the woman's name? Why, oh why, had he thrown the damn thing away?

'Marshal?' Bruno put his head round the door. 'I'm going to do the shopping, so if there's anything you want . . .' He stared in amazement at the growing heap of paper on the Marshal's desk.

The Marshal, catching his eye, growled, 'Somebody has to keep things in order round here.' And went on making a mess.

'Well, if there's nothing you want—'

'There's plenty I want but you won't find it going shopping! I want the name of that wretched woman who came in here saying her son was missing for a start!'

'That one you were annoyed about because we should have sent her away?'

'You don't mean you remember her?'

'Well, I remember because you were so annoyed—'

'Her name and address! What was her name and address?'

'That's what you were so annoyed about. That we didn't ask her, otherwise we'd have known to send her away.'

'Oh, for God's sake!' He went on with his useless rummaging.

'Have you nothing better to do than stand there?' he asked, since Bruno didn't leave.

'The shopping . . . but if you want I could call Scandicci and ask someone—'

'Scandicci?'

'That's where you said she should have reported—'

'Scandicci . . . silver, they made silver gifts! Well, don't just stand there. Go and do the shopping.'

'Yes, sir.'

'And don't call me sir.' But Bruno had got out at speed. He called Scandicci.

'Silverware? That must be Fossi.'

'That's it—I thought Fossi was the name of the street.'

'That's because they're in Via del Fosso. We have a Station just round the corner—'

'That's the one. Can you give me their number to save me time?'

The marshal of the tiny Station was out when he called but his brigadier knew the family well enough.

'Signora Fossi?' He laughed. 'You mean it's true that she came to you as she said?'

'Yes.'

'She said she had, but we hardly believed that even she would take her story anywhere but here.'

'You mean it wasn't true? The son wasn't missing?'

'Oh, as to that . . . He slides off every now and then and with a mother like that, who wouldn't? It depends what you mean by missing.'

'He came back just as usual?'

'Certainly he came back. Saw him myself in the bar this morning. The Fossi woman is our pet pain in the neck. She's round here every other day complaining about something and I don't know how many times she's reported her son missing. The first time we took her seriously, put him in the bulletin and everything, but after five or six episodes

we stopped bothering. Probably got a fancy woman somewhere, know what I mean?'

'Yes . . .' It was what he'd suggested himself, now he
remembered.

'God knows why she picked on you when we sent her
packing. You'd have thought she'd try the police or something.'

'She said I'd helped a friend of hers with some minor
problem.'

'And you sent her packing too, I imagine?'

'Yes, but I'm not so sure I was right. You say you saw
him this morning?'

'In the bar. He usually nips out for a coffee about ten and
so do I.'

'I'll come out there. Will the Marshal be back? Say in
about half an hour?'

'He'll be back well before then. I'll tell him. What was
the name again?'

'Guarnaccia.'

The traffic was heavy. It always was on that road which,
once you were out of Florence, was lined with factories.
Traffic lights one after the other, one of which he all but
went through on red because his mind wasn't on his driving.
It was on his conversation with that Fossi woman. She had
said a number of things which, at the time, hadn't made
much sense but which were beginning to. Her son's little
jaunts. She'd seemed to be defending them. Set in his ways,
she'd said, because he'd married late. And she was the
one who'd convinced him to marry. When the Marshal
had suggested another woman she'd said, 'Certainly
not. He doesn't go in for that sort of thing.' And she had
been quite certain, certain enough to be convincing. She
knew.

He didn't stay long at the sleepy little carabinieri station,
only long enough for a courtesy visit and directions to the
factory. When the marshal there offered to accompany him

he said, 'I'd rather go alone. I want it to look as casual as possible.'

'You really think . . .?'

'I don't know.'

'I can't believe it. I mean, he's such a respectable character . . .'

It was a new red brick factory. There were a number of them, some in brick, some in concrete, all of them incongruous eyesores in what was still an agricultural village. The green-painted iron gates of the silver factory stood open. A van and a small car were parked on the gravel near the main entrance. It was a small place with no porter's lodge. The man who noticed him and asked what he wanted was obviously one of the workmen. He left the Marshal waiting in what looked like some sort of showroom. There were shelves and shelves of silver ornaments, the sort of thing people gave as useless and expensive wedding presents.

'Can I help you?'

He turned and saw a blonde young woman whom he realized must be the daughter-in-law. She was expensively well-dressed and carefully made up, but in the split second before she spoke and offered him a businesslike smile, the Marshal saw a face that was unhappy, unhappy, but not frightened.

'I understand you wanted to speak to my husband?'

'Is he here?'

'I'm sorry, he's not. Can I be of any help—nothing's happened, has it? You're not here because—'

'No, no, don't worry.'

'I suddenly thought . . . a road accident . . .'

'No. Don't alarm yourself.' Although . . . He and the marshal round the corner had cooked up a story about a bag-snatching but a road accident would do just as well. 'As a matter of fact, there has been an accident but your husband wasn't in any way involved. I was hoping that he might come forward as a witness.'

'He never mentioned seeing an accident. Where did it happen?'

'Well, of course, it might be a mistake.' Perhaps he should have stuck to the bag-snatching. 'Someone took the number of a passing car but you know how these things are. They get the number wrong or the car turns out to be a different colour . . .'

With no further demur she gave him the number of her husband's steel-grey Mercedes. As he wrote it down she said, 'It's odd that he shouldn't have mentioned it.'

'Might have gone out of his mind—or—could he have told anyone else in the family when you didn't happen to be there? After all, there's no reason why he should do more than mention it in passing. He wasn't involved.'

'I suppose he could have told his mother . . .'

'Then perhaps I could have a word—unless you're expecting your husband back any minute, in which case . . .'

'No. He planned to have lunch with our agent and then they had business to discuss—that's not where it happened, by any chance? On Via Baracca? It's such a terrible road. I know Carlo always cuts through the park to avoid the worst of it.'

'It was in that area, yes.'

'Then I'm not surprised. I hate driving over there myself. Well, if you want to talk to my mother-in-law you can, but if you don't mind I'll have to get someone else to take you round to the house—she's already gone to supervise lunch and I have to take a client to the restaurant. I hope you'll excuse me.'

'Of course.' He was only too glad to excuse her. He had to talk to the woman alone.

The same man who had first greeted him took him out of the door he had first entered and round the side of the building to the two-storeyed house attached to the factory. The front door was opened by a very young maid and the grey-coated man went away.

'Will you wait here?'

The Marshal stood, hat in hand, in the entrance while the maid tapped on a door on the left and went in, leaving it ajar.

He heard the girl announce his arrival in a low voice but all he could see through the crack in the door was the end of a large table where the little girl with dark eyes and long blonde hair sat silent and still before an empty plate. He got an impression of chill formality despite what must have been an everyday family meal. There wasn't even the faintest smell of food. Then Signora Fossi appeared and closed the door behind her.

'Oh, it's you . . .' She was surprised and a flicker of fear crossed her face but she composed herself at once. She didn't ask him why he was there, gave him no lead at all, only waited, her eyes watchful.

'I've just spoken to your daughter-in-law.'

She was immediately alarmed. He saw a red flush appear on her neck and she opened her mouth to speak but thought better of it.

'I understand your son returned home.'

'He did. There was no need to have bothered you. I'm afraid I'm an anxious sort of person and my heart isn't all that strong. My son has the same weakness. He had rheumatic fever as a child.'

He understood that this was a plea for sympathy. She would have liked to say, 'Go away. Please go away and leave us in peace.' How much did she know? How much did she only suspect or fear? He didn't, he couldn't, feel any personal sympathy for this woman who appeared to him now even less prepossessing than at their first encounter. But the man was her son. He couldn't get away from the thought. Her son. And then there was the unhappy young wife. Of the silent child behind the closed door he tried not to think at all. He had to do his job and the steadily rising flush on the face and neck of the woman before him told him that his job lay here.

'I told your daughter-in-law I was looking for her husband as the possible witness to a road accident.' He gave her a moment to digest this before adding, 'The truth is that I think he may be a witness to something much more serious. I don't think I need to tell you what.'

He could see an enormous energy building up in her and despite his great bulk he felt she would have been capable of thrusting him bodily out of her home could there have been anything to be gained by it. She still didn't utter a word.

'I have to speak to him. In cases like this we use the utmost discretion. You told me you were very close to your son and I imagine you know all the facts about his private life, facts his wife may not be aware of. If he comes forward he'll be protected in that respect, his name won't be published. If he tries to run away . . .' He left the threat unspoken, watching for her reaction. It didn't come. His threat hadn't worked, he could see that, though he couldn't be sure why. He would have to lay it on thicker because it was plain that she was only waiting for him to leave so that she could act and her first act would be to telephone her son.

'I might as well be honest with you,' he lied. 'I must speak to your son at all costs. I have the number of his car and all stations and airports have been alerted. Don't do anything that will make things worse for him.'

A bead of perspiration formed near the grey hair on her temple and rolled down her powdered cheek. She didn't say a word. From behind the dining-room door came the faint chink of cutlery. The solitary child was eating.

CHAPTER 9

He pulled up, leaving the engine and wipers on and switched on the radio. 'Anything?' The rain hammered on the car roof.

'No sign of him yet.' The Marshal's colleague out in the village sounded excited. The Marshal himself was subdued.

'He should have got there by now. He left Via Baracca a good twenty minutes before I arrived, without finishing his business.'

'His mother did call him, then?'

'He received a call. He took it in an office alone but I imagine it was her. You're sure he couldn't have approached his house—on foot, say—without your boys spotting him?'

'Impossible. I promise you he hasn't come back here. Where are you now?'

'Half way back. I've just stopped in the Piazza delle Cascine. It's the road he takes, so his wife said, and the people at the agency in Via Baracca confirmed it. Piazza Puccini, Via delle Cascine, then straight up through the park to Ponte alla Vittoria and the road out to Scandicci. It avoids all the traffic in the centre . . .' And he repeated, 'He should be there by now . . .'

'But he isn't. Listen, you know your own business best but have you thought of the station, the airport?'

'He thinks they're being watched.'

'He thinks . . . Well, as I say, you know your own business best. There's nothing much we can do here except go on waiting and watching.'

'Yes. Thank you.'

'No need to thank me! I must confess we're rather enjoying it. The last time anything happened round here was when Nardi's pig escaped and that was nearly two years ago!'

'Keep in touch, every ten minutes or so.'

'Right—Wait a minute. I've thought of something. It's only just crossed my mind but Fossi may well be armed.'

'A pistol?'

'That's right. He has a licence, all regular. It's because of their having so much valuable stock.'

'Then surely he keeps it somewhere in the factory?'

'Most of the time, yes. But I know he goes armed when

he's delivering stuff to the buying agency because their insurance only covers it from the moment it arrives in their hands.'

'I see. Thanks for the warning. He hasn't . . .'

'What's that?'

'I was just wondering . . . you said nothing much happens out there but has Fossi ever, by any chance, reported a theft of some sort?'

'He did once, yes, but not here. That was when he decided to apply for a licence to carry arms. Happened in the park somewhere, so he didn't report it here but I heard about it. I'm surprised he still uses that road, he'd have done better to take a more frequented route instead of going about with a gun he probably doesn't know how to use. Still, if I remember rightly they didn't get away with much.'

'I see.'

The Marshal broke radio contact and then called his own Station. It was Bruno who answered.

'Is Ferrini back?'

'He's just come in. Shall I put him on?'

Ferrini's voice sounded faintly puzzled but he didn't ask any questions right away.

'They're fixing up the photos. They reckon they can have him presentable as a respectable member of society by tomorrow. Will that do? It takes a bit of time.'

'That's all right. Listen, I want you to call Carla—he won't be awake but let it ring until he is. Ask him . . . Ask him if in the days when Nanny went with him he ever paid, or tried to, with a present rather than money.'

'If I can wake him, I'll ask him. Anything else?'

'No.'

'But . . . Where are you?'

'In the park finding Nanny. At least, I think that's who I'm finding . . .'

'But how? I mean how did you—'

'Because of a dispute over two adjoining gardens up near

Via San Leonardo . . . It was all a long time ago and it's a long story. Call Carla for me, will you?'

'Right away. But don't you need any help?'

'I don't know. Perhaps. Stay where you are and I'll call.'

He stared out past the fast-clicking wipers at the dripping trees and the puddles around the edge of the tarred piazza. It was raining so hard that even in the early afternoon it was beginning to grow dark. The radio crackled into life again and Bruno's voice said, 'Marshal, your wife's in the office. I think she'd like a word with you.'

'Put her on.' He'd missed lunch again, and this time he hadn't even remembered to tell her.

'Salva? Are you all right?'

'Yes. I'm sorry. I didn't get a chance . . .'

'Today of all days, and I'd made something special. Well, I can save it for supper, I suppose. You will come home?'

'I don't know.'

'But Salva, the boys—'

'I don't know. I don't know what will happen . . .' And his voice sounded so heavy and so distracted that she gave up and went away.

What did she mean, anyway, 'today of all days'? She'd sounded hurt. It was already something that she'd sought him out, given the way things were, and now he seemed to have upset her. He perhaps ought to call her back. But he didn't. He sat there, listening to the rain drumming on the roof of the car, brooding. Fossi had set out on this road. The man from the agency had seen him. They'd set out together and driven one behind the other as far as Piazza Puccini when Fossi had turned right and taken the road through the park. But he hadn't come out the other end. He knew he couldn't go home. And he was armed.

Ferrini interrupted his brooding.

'I've talked to Carla. He was like a zombie but I managed to get through the fog.'

'Well, was there ever a present?'

'More than once. Apparently his wife kept the purse strings so he didn't have much ready cash to play with. He once gave her a silver fruit bowl, that was all. Lulu, on the other hand, screwed quite a few presents out of him and wanted money as well.'

'What presents exactly?'

'I don't know. Knick-knacks of all sorts—'

'But silver?'

'Yes, silver, fairly valuable.'

When the Marshal made no answer, he asked, 'That is what you wanted to know?'

'Yes. I wasn't sure, you see . . .'

'You're all right, are you? I can come straight down there if—'

'No. No . . . at least, yes, come as far as the entrance near the Ponte alla Vittoria. Bring somebody with you. I'll call you in if anything turns up.'

'We could call in more cars, comb the whole park area . . . dogs . . .'

'No.'

'What if he should be armed?'

'I think he is.'

'Then surely all the more reason—'

'No.'

Ferrini, realizing he was talking to a brick wall, agreed to come down as far as the entrance and wait.

The Marshal put his little black car in gear and moved off slowly. The man had driven in here and never come out at the other end. He probably had a pistol. A respectable man with an ingenuous wife. A little girl who had finished her lonely meal and was doing her homework. They knew Carlo Fossi but they didn't know Nanny. Nanny who had walked back into Lulu's flat to take his clothes and retreat to the world of Carlo Fossi, only to find . . . What? To know that, he had to find Nanny. Perhaps there wasn't much time and yet he drove very slowly. His head told him to hurry, that if Nanny had remained in the dripping, deserted park it was because he didn't intend to live long enough to be Nanny the witness. He wanted to die as Carlo Fossi. And still the Marshal drove slowly, feeling as heavy and dispirited as the sodden, dripping trees around him. Another call came from the watchers of Fossi's house. Nothing.

He was driving at random. He passed the Little Zoo. Once they had taken the boys there to see the scurrying hairy baby pigs and the chattering monkeys. Now the place was gloomy and deserted, the sandy enclosures empty and full of puddles, the animals sheltering somewhere from the relentless rain. His windows were steaming up. He wound one down a crack and drove on. He passed the racecourse. The rain here was heavy with the smell of horse dung but there was neither horse nor man in sight. When he reached the end of this avenue he would be at the Indian, where they had sat the other day looking at the river. The end of the park. There he could turn and drive up the next avenue. But before he reached the Indian he braked very gently and reversed to the right, sliding the car on to a bumpy patch of grass among untended bushes. He switched off the engine. He had seen the tail-end of a car, parked like his own, off the road in the bushes. A large steel-grey car. He got out, leaving his door loose to avoid noise, and moved forward through the tangle of wet brush. The rain covered the noise of his footsteps, the wet gloom of the dreary afternoon half hid him. He drew level with the boot of the car that had pulled off on the opposite side of the road. A steel-grey Mercedes, the number plate he was looking for, and a grey-suited figure slumped forward over the steering-wheel.

For some time the Marshal stood there motionless in the rain. Carlo Fossi dead would mean the little blonde girl need never know . . . But Peppina? What would happen to Peppina? Then he gave a start. The slumped figure had surely moved, the shoulders had just perceptibly lifted. The Marshal took a step back and concealed himself better.

The shoulders moved again and then the head was flung back against the headrest. The greying fair hair was a little too long. The figure settled and once again became motionless. The Marshal waited, trying to think of a way out for Peppina if what he thought might happen did happen.

With a shock he saw the figure jerk upright. The car door opened and the man got out. He seemed to be in a daze and walked unsteadily as though he'd been sitting stiffly for too long. It was too gloomy to make out more of his face than that it was thin. He walked round to the boot and opened it, took out some sort of hold-all and walked away from the car, leaving both the door and the boot wide open.

The Marshal moved forward cautiously, not understanding. Maybe he was making for the river. Maybe he didn't have the gun with him after all, but the hold-all? He was forced to pause at the end of the bushes where the gravel space around the Indian opened before him. There was no more concealment. But the man had vanished.

There had been no cry, no splash, and surely no time for him to have reached the river bank. Where could he be hidden—unless he was simply standing behind the big monument? The Marshal gave up concealment and walked forward towards the turbanned prince under his pagoda-like shelter. He walked round to the other side. An empty bench. Wet gravel, a view of the swollen river. Nothing else. Then, from the right, he heard a voice.

Was that it? Had he arranged to meet somebody? He began to walk across the gravel towards the sound. There, near a footbridge crossing the Mugnone Torrent, a dry ditch in summer but swollen and racing now, stood a dilapidated yellow building that had once been a coffee-house but had been out of use for years. The voice was coming from in there, urgent but not angry. He couldn't make out the words. The first window he found was boarded up so he made for the front of the building, thinking all the time of that hold-all. The saw? Lulu's bloodstained clothing? The front door was also boarded up and the whole of the façade was plastered with tattered posters and sprayed with graffiti.

'*In this world of thieves and scoundrels, we are squatting . . .*' A huge handwritten notice, partly obliterated by the rain. '*Since 1975 this building has been scheduled for renovation. Years have passed and the Left-wing alliance . . .*'

The Marshal had a vague recollection of some group claiming to be anarchists occupying the place until some trouble with the police had put an end to their stay. There must be some way in. The voice stopped and then started up again in a different tone—or was it a different voice? A false drawl about it, close to the softened male voice of a transsexual but not the real thing. Quietly, he returned to his car and called Ferrini. 'Don't come in there. Wait outside.'

He stumbled over clumps of soaked grass, a collapsed armchair with a puddle in its sagging seat, a pile of tin cans. There was another, smaller door hanging loose on its hinges. The place had probably been used by tramps after the squatters. He stepped inside and, adjusting his eyes to the deeper, windowless gloom, found himself in a tiny theatre.

Facing him on a low platform was a small cinescreen with a dark rent in the centre of it. Two dozen or so low armchairs probably left over from the days of the coffee-house were lined up in front of it. The peeling, dusty walls were stuck all over with old photocopied sheets of information and big handwritten posters full of giant exclamation marks like the one outside. It was too dark to see what they said. There was only one source of light and that a feeble one. It came from the crack beneath a small battered door on the other side of the room. Behind the door the voice or voices continued their earnest talk which the Marshal could now make out better.

'Of course I shan't go away. I can't go away now, can I? Now that you've seen to everything. Tell me you like this dress. You always did like it. Tell me it turns you on. It does, doesn't it? I can see by your eyes! Tell me!'

The Marshal pushed the door gently.

The light was coming from a big electric torch standing upright on the filthy floor. He recognized the dress at once. The glittering trail of sequins, the plunge from shoulder to waist. He recognized the stance, too. The face turned towards him over a raised shoulder, one hand on the hip, the black hair swinging behind. And most of all, the fixed, dazzling travesty of Lulu's famous smile.

The Marshal's quiet entrance seemed to create no disturbance. The glittering figure, lit theatrically from below, twirled provocatively for his benefit, then stopped, laughing softly.

'You should say you like my dress, you adore it. That's what Nanny would say. If you kicked him in the teeth he'd only look at you like a beaten dog and say "I worship you"— in a voice just like that—"I worship you, Lulu!" Can you imagine?'

'Can I talk to him?'

'To Nanny? Suit yourself. You'll find him a bore but I can't leave him now, you understand that?'

'Yes.'

The room must have served as some sort of dressing-room or perhaps even a bedroom in the days of the anarchists. Most of it appeared deep in shadow because of the torch which illuminated the tall figure and a circle of grimy ceiling above where a broken electric cord dangled. Then the torch was snatched up from the floor and placed on a cluttered little table with a spotted mirror propped at the back of it. The figure seated itself and the black hair fell in a heap on the table like a crouching animal. The face dimly reflected in the mirror was still caked with make-up but framed now by a straggle of fair greying hair. The eyes reflected to the Marshal's gaze were haggard and the brilliant smile was gone as though wiped away. He was looking now at Nanny.

'I had to talk to you,' the Marshal said.

'I know.' He rubbed a weary hand over his face, blurring the make-up. 'My mother told me.' This was another voice, low and defeated. 'What do you want from me?'

The Marshal stood very still. He couldn't see his own reflection but Nanny could see it and responded to it without turning to face him. 'It's about Peppina. Peppina's in prison, did you know that?'

'Oh yes. I read it in the paper.'

'He's accused of killing—of murder.' He was afraid to name Lulu in case she reappeared. The eyes in the mirror watched him in silence. He was forced to go on.

'Peppina claims you took him to Lulu's flat.'

'Why should I do that?'

'We know he was there. We took fingerprints. I expect we'll find yours among them as well as his.'

'Of course. I was staying there.'

'And you took Peppina there.'

'No.' The eyes narrowed in thought and then he said, 'She came there on her own.'

'And you let him in?'

'Why not? And I left her there. I went away.'

He could hardly avoid it now.

'Where was Lulu?'

'She was there. Lulu was there.'

'And you left? And then Peppina murdered Lulu?'

'That's what must have happened. Peppina hated her.'

'So did a lot of people.'

'They didn't understand her.'

'But you did?'

'I loved her.'

The eyes in the mirror glittered and the thin lips flickered with the trace of a smile like a serpent's tongue. He raised a hand to one shoulder and followed the sagging contours of the sequinned dress down to the waist. 'Beautiful . . .' he whispered, 'perfect . . .' He was no longer talking to the

Marshal's reflection but to his own as he repeated, 'I loved her.'

And the Marshal knew then that this wasn't a missing witness he'd found, but a murderer. He also knew that no one else would ever see what he was seeing, that there would be no Nanny in the witness-box but a respectable businessman named Carlo Fossi, surrounded and supported by his mother and a lot of expensive lawyers. A respectable man tricked and corrupted and set up by a social pariah known as Peppina.

Unless he confessed. And the only time for a confession was here and now. In measured tones he said, 'But Lulu didn't love you.'

The eyes jerked back into focus.

'That's a lie. You know nothing about it. You don't know Lulu.'

'Lulu didn't love you or anybody else. Lulu loved Lulu, Lulu's body, Lulu's money. Did you think you could keep it up without money? You had no money you could get at, did you? You moved in but sooner or later the truth had to come out. That you'd brought no money with you. Is that what went wrong?'

'I loved her. Why didn't she understand? What was money compared to what I'd given up for her? Everything! I gave up everything! For years I'd worked, building up a business. I gave it up. My mother, my wife, my home . . . I left everything because I loved her. Why didn't she understand? She laughed in my face. She said I was crazy. I'd laid my whole life at her feet and she laughed at me. Over a year it had taken . . . sometimes she'd let me stay a day or two, then she'd kick me out. You had to understand her. There was a wild streak in her but I loved that too, I worship everything about her. Why didn't she understand? Why?'

'Did she ask you for money?'

'The rent. Three million. I had nothing—I'd given up

everything for her but she couldn't see it. I've thought a lot about it. I thought: She's never had any real love offered to her in her life, so she can't understand. I thought . . . I must be patient. I was humble, I offered to leave, to let her think it over. She was bound to miss me, do you see? If I could manage to stay away from her long enough, she'd realize. No! Oh no!' It was Lulu's voice again. 'No, no, you creeping half-wit! That's not part of the bargain. I haven't put up with your creeping and whining for over two weeks so that you can slide off without coughing up a penny! You're not going anywhere except to the bank, and if you think you can crawl back home to your silly bitch of a wife you can think again! It's too late! They won't let you in the door after the nice little parcel I sent them!' He burst into a raucous laugh that went on and on until the voice was spent. Then with a faint sob the head fell forward. The crown, reflected in the mirror, was slightly bald. The Marshal waited, afraid to interrupt, until the eyes were slowly raised to his reflection again.

'I had to be patient. I had to work things out. She wanted me to sell the business, she wanted all of it. I couldn't . . . it wasn't so simple—I'd have done it, I'd have given her every penny I had in the world if only I could have undone what she'd done! But it was too late.'

'Your identity card?'

'Not just that. That was missing but there was a photo missing too, of me . . . a photo . . . And a letter, a letter describing things . . . details . . . she told me. She told me what she'd written and that she'd sent it . . .'

'To your mother?'

He shook his head and dropped his face into his hands.

And yet he'd been so sure that the wife . . .

Slowly, the figure seated at the mirror turned. The smeared and haggard face in the hard torchlight looked like an illuminated death's head. The lips barely moved as he whispered:

'To my little girl.'

Then he wept, his hands hanging loosely between his knees.

The Marshal, waiting for the crisis to pass, took stock of the room as best he could without moving. The only door was behind him, though he had few fears of the broken creature before him attempting to run away. He eventually spotted what he was looking for down by the side of the table. The hold-all was there with Carlo Fossi's suit draped over it. On top of the clothes lay a gun.

The weeping was beginning to subside. The limp hands sought each other and began turning over and over, the nails of one hand tearing at the back of the other.

'I need to wash. I need to wash my hands.'

'Not here. There's nowhere . . .'

'She used to mock me. She'd say, "Washing off the guilt?" especially when I was getting ready to go home. It's a need I have . . .' He had drawn blood from the backs of his hands but still he went on tearing. 'A need . . . it does nobody any harm, does it?'

'No.'

'She used to mock me. I had to destroy her, you understand that, like you have to destroy a dog that gets rabies even though you love it. You have to. But I had to be very careful. A child can forget things, after all, don't you think? The important thing was that she shouldn't grow up knowing her father was a murderer. I thought for a long time. Lulu imagined I was trying to sell the business but I wasn't. I was thinking. I thought if I wrote a letter to my little girl, telling her . . . telling her it was all lies and that because of it I'd been driven to suicide. She might have felt sorry for me. She might have believed me, mightn't she?'

'Perhaps.'

'She's so fragile, innocent . . .' To the Marshal's relief he stopped tearing at his hands and reached down towards his clothes.

The Marshal stiffened but made no move to stop him. The gun tumbled to the floor but Nanny appeared not to notice it. He fumbled in the pocket of his jacket and then turned back, holding out a photograph of the blonde child.

'You see.'

'She's very pretty.'

'Do you have any children?'

'Two boys.'

'Then you understand . . .' He took the photograph back and balanced it on his knee, gazing at it while he talked.

'My gun was at the factory, you see, so I couldn't . . . I thought of the river or even the bell tower. But I knew I'd never have the courage. Perhaps I wouldn't have had the courage even with the gun, I don't know. So I thought the best thing was to destroy Lulu first and then I would feel better and decide what to do. I thought of Peppina afterwards.'

'Why Peppina? What harm had she done you?'

'She hadn't done me any harm. She was just the first of them I came across.' He sounded surprised at the question. His gaze remained fixed on the photograph, on the pure, irrefutable reason for what he had done.

'The main thing was to destroy Lulu. I chose the night before she went to Spain. That way nobody would miss her for a long time, and anyway, it made a good excuse, don't you think? To prepare our last supper . . .' He frowned. 'I didn't want to use her sleeping pills. I would have liked her to be awake, you see. To know what I was doing so that she'd have to repent it. I wanted to make her understand . . . But I couldn't risk it. Lulu was strong and fought like a wildcat, so . . . Even then, when I put her in the bath and hit her head with the rolling-pin I thought the pain would wake her and then . . . But it didn't. I hit her and hit her but she never woke up. She was dead and I hadn't been able to make her understand the evil she'd done. But I felt better, even so. I felt better . . .' He stroked the little face in the photograph delicately.

'What did you do then?'

'I filled the bath. I had to, you see, or the body would have become rigid and I wanted to deal with it afterwards. After I'd been out and organized an alibi. I filled it with warm water. Then I washed myself in the kitchen. I had to wash my hands. And I changed my clothes and left them in the bathroom and then I went out.'

'And you brought Peppina back so that her fingerprints would be in the flat.'

'Yes, and I gave her some of Lulu's traveller's cheques. I said Lulu had gone to Spain and forgotten them. I'd hidden the suitcase, I thought of that. I only thought of the traveller's cheques because Peppina told me, when we were having a drink, that she was saving to start a business. She was a fool to take them, wasn't she?'

'Yes.'

'But it was lucky for me. She went in the bedroom, too, before we left, to powder her nose, so you'll find her fingerprints there too.'

'And you went in the bathroom.'

'The water was all red. I told her, "I have to get rid of Peppina but I'll be back, Lulu." I felt very calm then so I didn't say it angrily, just "I'll be back."'

He fell silent, gazing down at the photograph, a different, softer expression in his face as though he were remembering a long-dead child instead of a living one.

The Marshal, too, remembered. He remembered a little girl who had aroused his empathy because for a moment they had shared the same sense of guilt mingled with satisfaction at the sight of a child who seemed so much less fortunate and who had cried because she couldn't have a pink satchel.

'Why did you go back?' he asked. 'Why? If you intended to kill yourself why did you . . . go on with it?'

But still the man stared down. 'She had my eyes, you know. I never wanted to marry—my mother . . . She had my eyes but her hair was almost white like her mother's. I never touched her. These hands . . . I never once touched her, only looked at her. I felt I couldn't, you see. And she would say, "Play with me. Papa, why won't you play with me?" I'd tell her, "Papas don't play, they have to work"— because I would never touch her with these hands. "I'll buy you a present," I'd say to her. "Tell me what you'd like most in all the world." Time and time again I'd ask her, "Tell me what you'd like most in all the world," and she . . . She'd think for such a long time and then ask for some trifle, so seriously. "I want a new pencil with pink and white stripes." And then she'd look at me to see if that would satisfy me. You see, she didn't really want anything. She had to think of something, she understood in her childish way that it was I who needed . . . And she was so innocent she never thought of taking advantage. Innocent—I had no business to be near such a creature, I know that. I always knew it. I lived in fear that one day I'd lose the right to even so much as look at her, the way I used to do when she was sleeping. Anyone would have had the right to take her away from me—but not to defile her, not to dirty her!' The hands holding the photograph gripped it tight, trembling. 'Lulu had to be destroyed. She had to be punished. When I came back I decided what to do. I felt very calm and decided . . . But I had nothing to do it with, you see, so I went to bed. First I emptied the bath and put some very hot water in it because of what I had to do. Then I was hungry and I ate some of the food that was left. And then I slept.'

'Where did you buy the saw?'

'From an ironmonger. I drove across town in the morning and found a shop a good distance away, I don't remember the street. I chose it badly, it should have been bigger. It was all right for the neck and the arms but it wasn't long enough and the flesh on her thighs was too thick. It got caught a few times. It took me a long time because it was so difficult. It was the end of the saw, you see, that would bury itself in the flesh. It should have been longer—it caught in her dress as well until I thought of taking it off.'

The Marshal's stomach felt tight and cold, not because of what he was being told but because of the manner of telling. It might have been a game of cards he was describing.

'When I'd finished I put some of the pieces in plastic rubbish bags and some in a suitcase because there weren't enough bags. I couldn't take them out to the car until it went dark, so I spent all day cleaning the bathroom. I cleaned it and cleaned it until every trace of her was gone. I stuffed the bloodstained clothes and towels and rags in plastic bags and then I packed my clothes.'

He stopped and looked up at last. He looked straight at the Marshal and began to laugh. 'I packed my clothes! And there in the top of her wardrobe I found my identity card and the photograph! She'd made it all up, you see! Everything was all right—all I had to do was get rid of the bags and I could go home. I opened one of them—one of the bags—and put the photo in it—you didn't find it, did you?'

'No.'

'So, you see, everything's all right. I dumped the bags in a lot of different places and then it was all over.' He gave a deep sigh of weary satisfaction 'All over . . . I feel so tired.'

His gaze was drifting, his mind so evidently giving up the struggle to hang on to sanity that the Marshal said quickly, 'It's over for you, yes. But I have to arrest you now. You've confessed to the murder of Lulu and I have to arrest you.'

He only looked confused and didn't speak.

'You'll be tried. It'll be in all the papers. I'm sure your wife and your mother will do all they can to protect your little girl, but sooner or later she'll find out. Fossi, do you understand what I'm saying to you? I have to arrest you.'

The tired eyes stared back at him without expression. The Marshal looked at the gun still lying on the floor.

'I'm going outside for a moment,' he said, 'and then I'm coming back in with my men.'

He turned and walked out through the little theatre and opened the broken door. Ferrini was waiting with Lorenzini and young Bruno, the three of them huddled as close to the building as possible in a hopeless attempt to shelter from the beating rain.

'You can come in,' he told them.

CHAPTER 10

'Sweet Jesus.' Ferrini looked into the torchlit room over the Marshal's broad shoulder.

The Marshal himself said nothing. Both the gun and Nanny were exactly as he had left them. They took him away, Ferrini leading the way out with the torch, the two younger men flanking the handcuffed prisoner. The Marshal retrieved the bag with the gun and clothing. As they left the darkened room, Nanny hesitated and looked behind him.

'Lulu . . .?'

Then he went with them quietly.

When they got out of the car at Borgo Ognissanti they covered Nanny's shoulders with his jacket. He might have seemed a comic enough figure as they led him along the corridors in his trailing evening gown of sequins showing, in spite of the jacket, a muscular male chest, his men's black shoes treading heavily, his thin face smeared with make-up. But though a few of the uniformed men they passed turned to stare after them, not one of them, seeing the big drooping hands, the head which sagged as though he no longer knew how to hold it upright, the haunted eyes, seemed inclined to laughter.

For almost three hours people bustled around him, asking questions, photographing him, fingerprinting him, taking him from room to room. He continued silent and quiescent. When they showed him the typed version of his confession he hesitated, unsure what they wanted. When they asked him if he understood what was happening he nodded. When they asked him to read the statement through he stared at it to oblige them. When they asked him to sign it he signed. His hand was shaking. Only once did he interrupt the voices around him to say that he wished to wash his hands. Thinking that he needed to relieve himself, they took him to the lavatory.

When they put the handcuffs back on him and he understood that they were going to lock him up, he searched the faces around him until he found that of the Marshal and asked, 'Will they let me see her one day, before I die?'

The Marshal understood that he meant his little girl but didn't know what to answer.

There was still a lot he had to go through. Lawyers, the Instruction, trial and appeal. But throughout it all and throughout the rest of his life until he died in prison, Nanny was never to speak again. Nor was he ever to see his child.

The Marshal arrived home that night to find the house in darkness. He switched on the light in the entrance and stood there in his wet clothes, sick at heart and drooping with tiredness. He had no idea what time it was. The light dazzled his eyes and he felt sore and aching all over. Then the bedroom door opened and Teresa was there, holding her dressing-gown around her.

'Salva,' she murmured, her face anxious, 'I waited up for you.'

He had no words to tell her how grateful he was. It was all he could do to move wearily towards her and reach out.

She held him without speaking until he relaxed his hold. Then she moved back a little to look at him.

'Salva, your clothes are soaked through . . . Whatever's happened? You look terrible.'

'I don't feel so good,' he admitted.

'Have you not eaten all day?'

'I don't know . . . No . . . perhaps at lunch-time . . . No, no I haven't.'

'Get out of those clothes and then come in the kitchen.'

He did as he was told.

Once in his thick dressing-gown in the still warm kitchen, he sat himself down and let Teresa make a place for him at the table which seemed to be covered in plates and dishes with silver foil over them. He ate everything she gave him hungrily, though he refused wine, and only when he was all but sated did he take notice of the number of elaborate dishes on offer.

Without total conviction he said, 'It's not Sunday.'

And she laughed at him and said, 'Salva, you're the absolute limit, you really are! It's your birthday.'

'Is it?'

'Why do you think I was so disappointed when you said you wouldn't be home to lunch? And then I got it all ready again tonight . . . You are a comic. Sit still, I've got something to show you.'

She went off to the sitting-room and came back with a rather clumsily wrapped parcel that looked to have more sticky tape than paper in the making of it.

'You've bought me a present?'

'Open it and see.'

It took him some time to unstick it all and when he'd succeeded he stared in puzzlement at the contents.

'It's for your desk, to put papers in.'

It was an oblong tray made of thin wood and covered all over with some sort of red, velvet-like paper. Glue had played as heavy a role in the lining as sticky tape had on the parcel. There was an envelope, too, from which he took a brightly-coloured birthday card. Inside it said, 'Happy birthday from Totò.'

For the first time in days a little smile lit his face.

'He made it himself? For me?'

'At school. You can't imagine how long it took him, he's so clumsy with his hands.'

'Like me.'

'He was so afraid he wouldn't have it ready in time. He overdid it a bit with the glue.'

'Yes.'

'There's a little something for you from me and from Giovanni too, but they can wait until tomorrow when you're rested. Let's go to bed.'

When they were settled and the light was out, she sensed that he was lying awake beside her.

'Can't you sleep?'

'I'm all right. I was just thinking . . .'

'Think tomorrow. You're worn out.'

'Yes, but . . . All that time . . .'

'What?'

'All the time that Totò was going through . . . He was working on my present . . .'

'Ever since term began.'

'And I thought, I really thought, that day he attacked me that he hated me. If you'd seen his face . . .'

'Salva! He's only a child. He loves you—if anything, he's more attached to you than to me, even though Giovanni looks so much more like you . . . It's funny. It's because he loves you that he reacted so strongly. He was so upset and a child can't always sort out the difference between love and hate.'

'Perhaps adults can't either . . . And all the time he was making me a tray.'

'Of course.'

'I'll never understand people. You . . . Teresa, I wish I'd let you talk to the Luciano woman.'

'I would have done, if you'd let me. It must have been a terrible shock for her.'

'It was. Perhaps she didn't mean the things she said.'

'What did she say?'

'It doesn't matter, now. You'll call her, will you?'

'I'll do it first thing tomorrow. But the boy . . . You should be the one to talk to the boy, Salva. Surely something can be done?'

'I'll try.'

She was right, of course. And the boy had come looking for him, frightened, and had been sent away. He'd done everything wrong, clumsy as usual . . . all that glue . . . He was no good with his hands and people were laughing at him as he tried to push them through the grille but they were too big. The cat thrust its head at him, purring, but he was too clumsy to help. He'd used as much glue as he could but where did glue come into it anyway? He must be falling asleep, that's what it was. He'd have to try again tomorrow.

'Have you seen the mother?' Ferrini asked.

'Just long enough for her to give me a nasty look. She talked to the Prosecutor.'

'The wife didn't come?'

'No. She took the first available plane to Finland with the child.'

'Can't say I blame her. Well . . .' Ferrini pushed his chair back and lit up. 'I think that's about it. A case brilliantly solved according to the manual. At least, that's how it will look to the instructing judge now that we've written him a good script.'

Ferrini and the Marshal had completed their reports in a borrowed office at Borgo Ognissanti, working, once again, late into the night. The Marshal was hunched over the mound of papers, looking gloomy.

'You could be a bit more cheerful. We've done a good job.'

'Sorry. It's this business of Peppina.'

'Oh, come on, the worst it can come to is receiving. He'll get off lightly.'

'I know—but he'd planned to get out, to give up prostitution, and now . . .'

'Listen, Marshal, I don't want to speak out of turn but I don't think you should give too much credence to what that sort tells you. They'll all give you hard luck stories and say they want to get out, but believe you me, they never do it, or not more than one in a million. You don't find that amount of tax-free money working in an office, you know.'

But the Marshal was unmoved. 'Nobody would have them in an office. Anyway, Peppina was hoping to set up a little fashion business. He'd got as far as signing on to do the exam at the Chamber of Commerce. I talked to him this morning. He's already scared to death of turning up for the exam even though they've no legal excuse to refuse him.'

'Hm. Well, I admit that if he's signed on for it that sounds a bit more convincing. Anyway, if you feel that strongly about it why don't you try getting the Prosecutor to drop the charge? You've got him in the palm of your hand right now. He's had his picture in the paper three days running.'

'I could try.'

'Try. After all, it's thanks to you that the business of the traveller's cheques has been dropped as far as Carlo Fossi's concerned.'

'And rightly so.'

'Rightly so, if you like, but it could have been pursued.'

'It would have been useless cruelty. He's already got so many aggravating circumstances against him, malice aforethought, use of a poison, damage to the corpse. He's only got one life to spend in prison, and it won't be a long one either. It seems his mother was telling the truth about his bad heart.'

'I agree with you. I doubt he'll ever set foot out of prison except for his trial. But, given the motive, I wouldn't be surprised if he got very little more than the minimum twenty-one years while if the Prosecutor tried for the profit motive . . . Well, as you say, he's only got one life— That reminds me, how's young Bruno?'

'All right but quieter.'

Bruno, who had been like a kid playing Cowboys and Indians from the day they found Lulu's remains until the night of the arrest, had grown up apace when stricken by the sight of the criminal he'd been so enthusiastically chasing. A sawn-up body had failed to shock him but the broken travesty of a human being which had once been Carlo Fossi had both moved and frightened him. He was now, as the Marshal said, quieter.

'I think I will talk to the Prosecutor, if you feel it's worth it.'

'I'm sure it's worth it—but try not to take it too much to heart if it doesn't come off. They're not the sort of people you can help because they don't help themselves. I know a good many of them and the only one with any sense is Carla —but even he doesn't get out, though he's been talking about it for years.'

'It can't be an easy decision,' the Marshal pointed out, 'to have the final operation, especially for someone like Carla who seems to have found some sort of equilibrium at the half-way stage. How can anyone know how they'd feel . . . afterwards.'

'There's some truth in that. It's not the real reason, though, if you ask me. Do you know what I think? I think it's a sort of arrogance—unconscious maybe, but it's there. They don't think they're something less than a real woman, they think they're something more because they've been brought up in a culture dominated by men and they won't be in any hurry to give up the three or four extra ounces that entitles them to keep one foot in the winning camp.'

'You think so?' The Marshal pondered a moment. 'It hadn't crossed my mind, I must admit.'

'Only an opinion—and you'd better not bring it up with the Prosecutor when you're making your appeal for Peppina!'

'I wouldn't dream—' But Ferrini was laughing at him.

'I wasn't serious. You have to laugh in this job or it gets you down. By the way, there's a rumour going about . . .'

'A rumour?' Was he joking again?

'About a promotion. Well, don't tell me if you don't want to, of course.'

'There's nothing to tell.'

'You don't mean you turned it down?' Ferrini's face was incredulous.

The Captain's face had been equally incredulous.

'You understand you may never get such a chance again?'

'Yes.'

It was possible now for a non-commissioned officer to be offered a commission if he showed particular aptitude. The Marshal had not only rejected the idea out of hand, he had appeared positively horrified. The Captain had talked to him at some length but hadn't succeeded in making him budge an inch.

'I can understand your reluctance. You have a family and, of course, you'd have to leave them for some time. Even so . . .'

He found himself, as so often happened with Guarnaccia, talking to a blank wall. The Marshal was glad he understood about not wanting to leave his family after all the years he'd had to wait to have them with him in Florence! He wasn't going anywhere, not even if they made him a general, never mind a lieutenant. That's what made him reject the idea out of hand. What horrified him was something else. There was some studying involved, exams! No, no . . .

'No, no . . .' he said again, now, shuddering at the thought.

'You mean you *didn't* turn it down?'

'No, I mean I did. I think we've finished for tonight, don't you?'

'If you say so.' Ferrini stubbed out his current cigarette in the overflowing ashtray and switched off the desk lamp. He stretched himself and stood up. 'It's been a long day.'

'Yes.' But there was still something the Marshal had to do. He had to see the Luciano boy and was embarrassed to have to ask Ferrini where he was to be found. Having got the directions, he stood up himself and started getting into his coat, carefully avoiding Ferrini's cynical glance.

'A family from my home town . . . You know how it is . . .'

Ferrini made no comment but turned out the main light as they left.

The boy was sitting on a bench under a dark and dripping tree. If the Marshal's headlights hadn't picked up his pale, crossed legs he'd have missed him despite the white globes of the nearest lamp. He got out of the car and approached the seated figure.

'What do you want? I haven't done anything.'

His wig was damp and looked slightly askew. Above the bare legs and short skirt he was huddled as deeply as he could into an old windjammer.

'Don't you know who I am?'

'Oh . . . It's you.' But he didn't look the Marshal in the face. His glance strayed from left to right and back again anxiously, as if afraid that the Marshal's presence might frighten away potential clients, though none of the passing cars showed any sign of slowing down. The Marshal knew he was blocking the boy from view but he stood where he was, looking down at the huddled, shivering figure, his hands thrust deep in his pockets.

'Your mother's worried about you.'

The boy only shrugged, his eyes still swivelling. Could it be that he was expecting a pusher rather than a client?

'You could just give her a call. There's no need to give her your own number if you don't want to.'

'I haven't even got a phone.'

'Even so, you could—'

'No! You don't know what you're talking about!' He was staring straight up at the Marshal now. His painted face was grotesque, almost comic, but the eyes were desperate. 'You can't imagine—if she once gets me in her clutches again . . . It's taken me so long to get free and now I'm staying away!'

'Listen, your mother—maybe your mother can't help being what she is—'

'What do you mean by that? What do you mean—"what she is"? What do you know about it?'

'I only meant—'

'You've no right to say anything against her!'

'I wasn't—'

'She's my mother! You've no right . . .' He subsided, hugging the old jacket to him tightly.

'I didn't mean to offend you. I'm only trying to say that I understand you wanting to be independent. She knows, anyway, that you're alive and well. I've told her that. It was only natural that she should be worried. She hadn't seen you since just after your accident.'

'What accident?'

'She told me you'd had a car accident, that you were in plaster last time you went home.'

'There wasn't any accident,' the boy said sullenly. 'I had to hide the operation, that's why my chest was in plaster. I'd forgotten I'd said it was a road accident. I told her I'd broken a rib or some such story. It wasn't even plaster, it was a sort of brace thing. I bought it.'

'You mean—'

'What do you think I mean? I don't sit out here for my health, do I? Why don't you just go away and leave me alone? I've got my living to earn.'

'There are other ways of earning a living. Why don't you get out before it's too late? It's dangerous, you know that by now, and it's not too late for you.'

'It is. It is too late, now. I've started some hormone treatment. Nobody wants transvestites any more, that's why I had to get breasts done. I might as well go the whole hog. That way I can earn more and once I've got rid of my beard I'll be able to afford to have my face done. Then I can make as much as they do.' He glanced along the avenue where the queue of cars was moving slowly. 'I might even be able to afford a flat of my own one day. That's what I want.'

'And you don't want your mother taking money off you, is that it?'

'No, it's not! I'll send her some money when I get on my feet, you can tell her that if you want. It's not money, it's . . . all of it. That life . . . She used to leave me with all the kids. Once, the littlest kid got sick. It was in the middle of the night. It was only a baby and it went all rigid and screaming and then it died. I was eight years old, for Christ's sake, so what was I supposed to do? I tried to give it some water from a bottle but it screamed and screamed and then it died. When she came back she nearly killed me because I was asleep. What could I do if it was dead? I fell asleep . . . I decided then I'd get out as soon as I was old enough. I like my life the way it is now. Nobody expects anything off me except what they pay for and the rest of the time I don't exist for anybody. I'm free.'

The Marshal stood a moment, immobile, hands still in his pockets, staring down at the puny legs, the scruffy high-heeled shoes. There was some sort of truth, some sort of half-baked logic in what the boy said. If you were neither male nor female, just a toy for rent at certain hours, you were indeed nobody and free of human responsibilities.

'And what sort of freedom is it?' he insisted. 'The freedom to be chopped to bits by some crazy client, or catch Aids or die of an overdose? What sort of freedom?'

But the boy only stared hopefully at the passing head-lights.

'What does it matter?' he said. 'You have to die of something. In any case, when I've made enough money, I can always give it up. When I'm about thirty or something and my life's over I'll maybe give it up . . .' He stiffened as a passing car slowed down, but the driver must have spotted the Marshal's uniform and he didn't stop. The boy went on staring hopefully down the long, lamplit avenue where reflected lights moved in an almost unbroken rhythm along the wet black road.

The Marshal got back in his car and drove home.

When he got there he braked as quietly as he could, avoiding a noisy spray of gravel. He switched off the engine and lights and sat there, shoulders hunched, staring out at the darkness. He was so still he might have been asleep. But he soon shook himself and got out of the car, shutting the door gently so as not to disturb the complete silence around him. His heavy footsteps crunched towards the doorway, then stopped. Why was it so unnaturally quiet? He had to think for a while before he realized what it was. It had stopped raining. He looked up. The sky was black and dotted with stars. It was colder, too. Tomorrow would be clear and sunny. Tomorrow was Thursday, his day off. His footsteps crunched on, a little bit lighter now. Tomorrow, after lunch he could take a walk through the Boboli Gardens with Totò. Not the whole family, just himself and Totò, and though he knew himself too well to think they would talk much, they might, if they walked near the fish pond, surprise the others by bringing home the little orange and white cat.